PURR-SUASIVE WITCHES

A Wonder Cats Mystery Book 11

HARPER LIN

GINGERBREAD HOUSE

"Oh my gosh. That smells so good," my cousin Bea said as we walked to the café.

"Are you serious?" I replied. "You think *that* smells good?"

I sniffed the air and looked around to find the source that was enticing her. It had to be coming from the arts and crafts festival, which was starting today.

"It's intoxicating," she replied, smiling.

"Jake, your wife has taken her pregnancy too far." I shook my head. "What kind of altered dimension am I living in when my vegan cousin, whose mantra is 'Lips that touch beef won't touch mine,' is now salivating at the smell of an outdoor barbeque?"

"Would you like me to bring you some barbeque today?" he asked lovingly while slipping his arm around her waist, which had expanded slightly with the bump in her belly.

"Oh my gosh." I rolled my eyes. "You two are like a walking Hallmark Channel movie."

"Yes, I'd love some barbeque. How about some ribs with a side of cheeseburger?" Bea replied, her hands folded in front of her as if she had to pray for Jake to say yes.

"Hey, I want in on that action," I said. "Some ribs with a side of cheeseburger? Food of the gods. Make it two, Jake."

"All right." He smiled at Bea and kissed her on the cheek. Then she kissed him on the cheek. Then the next thing I knew, I was five paces ahead of them, talking to myself while they made out on the sidewalk like two teenagers.

"Gross," I shouted and shook my head as I continued to the café.

The Brew-Ha-Ha Café was my home away from home. It barely felt like work, since my boss was my Aunt Astrid and my coworker was Bea. However, I had to admit that things had been getting a little snug behind the counter since Bea started to show. We were all very excited about her and Jake expecting their first baby. I was hoping for a boy. There was just something about the idea of having a little guy wearing blue and playing with trucks and soldiers and getting dirty that appealed to me. I knew they both said the same thing: "As long as the baby is healthy, we don't care."

I gave the front door a good yank, and it opened wide even though the sign still read CLOSED.

"Good morning," I said to my aunt, who was also glowing with the knowledge that she was going to be a grandma in three months and two days. She had a countdown written on what used to be the Specials board.

"Good morning, Cath. Where is Bea?" Aunt Astrid asked.

"She's causing a scandal in the middle of the street, making out with Jake like the ship is going down," I said as I walked to the swinging kitchen door and leaned in. "Morning, Kevin!"

"Morning, Cath." Kevin Baker was the hottest baking commodity in Wonder Falls, and he was all ours. Also, standing in the open kitchen back door was the most familiar and lovely face.

"Treacle, how did you beat me here?" I asked my black cat telepathically.

"You were going too slow."

"Blame Bea." I smiled and held the kitchen door open for him to slink into the main room. He hopped up onto the windowsill and collapsed in a square of sunshine, his tail lazily hanging over the edge. These

days, being a witch in a small family of witches came easily. Everyone was happy, healthy, and looking forward to the arrival of Baby Greenstone. I walked back over to my aunt and gave her an affectionate pat on the back.

Finally, Bea walked in, looking all fresh and glowy, rubbing her belly, and smiling. It was no secret that Bea had always been as cute as a button. But now that she was expecting, her red hair was shinier, her eyes were brighter, her cheeks were rosier, and she was all smiles all the time.

"Good morning, honey. Good morning, baby," Aunt Astrid said to Bea's belly. "Grandma will make something special for you."

"Yum," Bea said.

"Aunt Astrid, you won't believe what Bea has convinced Jake to get her for lunch," I said as I began to move the napkin holders from the counter to the tables.

"What?" Aunt Astrid looked at Bea suspiciously.

"A slab of ribs with a cheeseburger chaser," I replied. "Thank goodness he's getting one for me too. I couldn't bear to let her dive into red meat headfirst without my full support."

Aunt Astrid gasped. "Bea, you are already wrapped around that baby's finger. Is Jake bringing you lunch here?"

"Yes."

"Oh, I'm going to get a picture of this." Aunt Astrid pulled her camera out of her pocket. Ever since Bea had announced she was expecting, my aunt had carried her camera around and snapped pictures of both of us, recording every image that had anything to do with the baby.

"I want a copy," I piped up.

"You are both acting like having cravings is something strange. I'm sure that even this will pass as soon as the baby is born. But if this little angel has a taste for ribs and a cheeseburger, that's what he or she is going to get," Bea said as she bumped me with her belly while scooting past me to get behind the counter.

"You might want to get some olive oil and lube up that belly of yours so you can slide back and forth behind the counter," I joked. "How many more months do you have?"

"Three more," Bea said.

"I think your doctor predicted the date wrong," I said, patting her bump. "If you start going into labor, just look to the floor, because that's where I'll be, having passed out."

"Hardy-har-har," Bea said. "And don't talk like that. You know I'm going to need you in the delivery room."

"What?" I choked on the air. I loved Bea as if she were my own sister. But the thought of being in the room with her and Jake while she was having the baby made my hands go numb with terror... and disgust.

"You, my mom, and me. We have to be together in order for the baby-birthing ritual to work and protect the baby as he or she enters the world," Bea whispered. She shrugged at me as if this was nothing more than picking up a puppy at the shelter.

"Aunt Astrid, can I participate in the baby-birthing ritual from the hallway?" I asked, making them laugh even though I was deadly serious.

Still, talk about the baby and names and the nursery was all fun. I was enjoying the idea of being that aunt who would put hexes on the bullies at school and teach the little guy how to study for a test without cracking a book, simple tricks that we witches were privy to. I was ready for babysitting, and even the idea of changing diapers didn't deter me. It was a happy time. Except when Bea was hungry. And that was pretty much anytime she didn't have food in her hand.

"Let this grandma-to-be fix you some hearty oatmeal with fruit and raisins and cinnamon and all those good things you like," Aunt Astrid fussed. "Cath, would you like some too?"

"No. I'm going to wait for lunch," I said, pointing to Bea. "And I've got my camera waiting." She stuck her tongue out at me while squeezing back and forth behind the counter. We all chatted about nothing in particular. The warm weather was bringing in a lot more foot traffic. We talked about getting a permit to have seating outside.

"Did you hear about that accident at that little cottage you always liked over on Peabody Street?" Aunt Astrid asked me.

"You mean the Gingerbread House?" I gasped. Over on Peabody Street was a Cape Cod–style house painted in brown and cream that looked as if it had been plucked out of "Hansel and Gretel" and dropped into Wonder Falls. Pretty red tulips sprang up every spring, yellow daisies overran the flower boxes in the summer, and lush orange maple trees surrounded the yard each fall. The driveway was cobblestoned. A stone chimney stood proudly on the north side of the house, and there was a matching gazebo connected by a stone path out in the back-yard. It was a house truly suitable for a witch like me. It had gone up for sale six months ago, but it was way, way, way out of my price range. Still, I loved to admire it.

"Yes. It's in the paper," Aunt Astrid replied,

pointing to the newspaper on the counter. "Seems there was a murder-suicide."

"What? There was a suicide in that adorable little house?" I balked.

"Oh, that breaks my heart," Bea said.

"I know. Who could be suicidal in that beautiful home?" I continued.

"Cath." Bea shook her head. "Suicide is never about what people have on the outside. It's what's missing on the inside."

"I know, Bea." I went and patted her hand.

As an empath, she took any tragedy like this to heart. I knew exactly what she was thinking. If only she had taken hold of the afflicted person before it was too late, she'd have instantly been able to spot the sickness of the heart and maybe, just maybe, been able to ease the sadness or remove the parasite causing it.

"According to the paper, there was some kind of love triangle." Aunt Astrid shrugged.

"Who killed who?" I asked as I turned the Closed sign to read Open.

"She killed him and then herself. No children," Aunt Astrid replied.

"Thank goodness for that," Bea said, patting her belly.

"They were newlyweds if I remember right," I

thought out loud. The Brew-Ha-Ha had been in operation in Wonder Falls for so long that we had a steady stream of regulars. When any of us saw an unfamiliar face, we instinctively welcomed them. And I remembered the couple especially, since they had bought the house I coveted.

"That's what the article said," my aunt replied.

"Gosh, that's really too bad. Now that house is back on the market, and I still don't have the money to buy it," I muttered. "Unless the price went down due to the circumstances of its sudden vacancy."

Bea looked at me as if she smelled something foul. I shrugged.

The little bells attached to the front door began to jingle, thankfully pulling the attention away from me and my covetous behavior toward the little Gingerbread House and putting it where it belonged: on our customers.

2

COBWEBS

Bea's specialty teas were in high demand along with Kevin's gourmet muffins, breads, and salads. The morning rush was always fun. Time flew. When we finally got a breather in between the before-work crowd and the lunchtime swarm, it felt like only fifteen minutes had gone by instead of three hours.

"Cath, honey, there was something I wanted to ask you to do for me. But what was it?" Aunt Astrid tapped her chin as she stared into space, changing the subject.

I knew what it was, but I didn't want to say it out loud. We had lovely summer solstice decorations that had to be pulled down from the storage space. That was my job, but I was putting it off due to the fact that after the wet weather of spring, the spiders always seemed to love our summer solstice décor and would congregate around the boxes. I needed a hazmat suit that covered me from head to toe before I'd go disturbing any arachnid dwellings.

"Cath, can you get those boxes of decorations down today?" My aunt read my thoughts. And that wasn't even her gift. She could see other dimensions besides this one like layers of tracing paper stacked over each other. As far as I knew, she hadn't developed the skill of reading minds... yet.

"I would, but I'm not wearing a hoodie," I said plainly.

"What does wearing a hoodie have to do with anything?" Bea asked.

"It covers my head," I said, rolling my eyes as if this was all the reply they needed.

They both looked at me as if I'd just announced I had seen a rhinoceros outside the bank kitty-corner from us.

"If I don't cover my head, I might get cobwebs in my hair. Or worse. You know? Worse?"

"Cath, I really want to get the place decorated. Once you are over your strange fit, please bring down those boxes," Aunt Astrid said as she took her seat at her favorite table next to the counter to start work on the books, receipts, and payments due.

"There are spiders up there. What if I get one on me? Just let me do it tomorrow," I protested.

"Thank you, honey. You are such a good employee," Aunt Astrid said as she went back to her books.

"I have an idea, Cath," Bea said as she slid herself out from behind the counter.

Before I could say no, she had me wrapped up in a makeshift raincoat made out of large garbage bags and duct tape.

"How do I look?" I asked her as I took hold of the latch that opened the storage space. It wasn't a very large door; it was just big enough for me or Bea—well, Bea prepregnancy—to squeeze into. The boxes were in just far enough that a person would have to kneel on the edge and lean their entire torso into the spider den.

"You look like the Terminator." She smiled. "Now go show those tiny, petrified, harmless little bugs who's boss." She clapped me on the back.

I wasn't happy. But I did as I was told. Within seconds, I had the first box in my rubber-gloved hands and was yanking it out of the space with relative ease. The second box was a little trickier, because it was set back farther. Of course it was. It was hung up on an uneven floorboard. It had to be. So I had to lean in farther.

"You okay?" Bea asked, and I could hear the laughter just behind her words.

"I'm fine," I snapped as I gave the box a good yank.

"You need any help?" Bea snickered.

"What are you going to do, Wide Load? Come in here and help. We'll be wedged in like sardines. I'll have an anxiety attack. The fire department will have to get us out with the Jaws of Life."

By this time, Bea was not trying to hide her laughter.

Finally, with one hard tug, I was able to free the box and pull it toward me. As usual, it was covered in cobwebs, but I did not see any living eight-legged devils on it. With a sigh, I lugged it out of the tiny space, hearing a gentle jingle of the decorations inside, and set the box on the floor. When I turned to face Bea, I saw her smiling proudly, about to speak, when her eyes focused on something that made her mouth fall open and her eyes bug out.

"Cath, don't move," she said.

"Why?" I was sure she was just teasing me. My aunt and cousin knew full well about my arachnophobia. Sure, it was a little over the top. Maybe I overreacted at times.

"Just let me get the broom," Bea said and dashed

into the kitchen, where the brooms and dustpans were.

I stood still and looked down the front of my garbage-bag suit and saw nothing. I looked over my arms and, aside from dust, saw nothing there, either. With confidence, I brushed away the hair that was tickling my cheek and reached to push in the kitchen door. Then I saw it. It hadn't been hair tickling my face. It was...a spider. The size of a hubcap. On my hand. It had just been on my face. And I hadn't known it.

Bea burst through the swinging kitchen door with a broom in each hand. "Don't move!" she shouted.

"What's going on back there?" Aunt Astrid called.

"Get it off me!" I screamed as I held my hand out, hoping the natural tremor in my body would shake the creature to the floor. But it clung to me as if I was the last life preserver on the *Titanic*.

"Hold still!" Bea raised one of the brooms over her head.

"I can't!" I squealed and violently shook my hand up and down, only to scare the thing into bolting up my arm in search of a safer place. I swept my other arm over my sleeve, trying not to touch the creature long enough for it to take hold of that limb. All the while, I was unaware of the fact that I was on tiptoes, hopping back and forth from one to the other.

"Why are you both shouting?" Aunt Astrid called from the dining area, but I couldn't answer her.

My voice went up about five octaves as I shouted to Bea. "Get it off me! Get it off me!"

"Hold still and close your eyes!" Bea said. I squeezed my eyes shut while still dancing on my toes, my arms held out straight as if I was doing an impersonation of Frankenstein's monster. Finally, I felt the brush of the broom across the left side of my chest and down my arm. I didn't dare open my eyes but instead opened my mouth to cry out like a toddler who didn't want to go to sleep.

"Okay! I got it!" Bea shouted.

I opened my eyes just in time to see the brown thing fall to the ground, its legs—which were as long as my fingers—splayed out around it. It froze there, and I knew it was looking at me.

"Ew! Ew! Ew! Ew!" I hopped, shivered, and ran to my Aunt Astrid. I tore at the duct tape that, thankfully, secured my rubber gloves tightly to the plastic bag Bea had fashioned around my arms and head. I tore at my homemade hazmat suit, paying no attention to the customers who were filling some of the tables and staring at me with amusement. I tried to catch my breath.

"Did you get my decorations?" Aunt Astrid asked, staring at me.

"Yes," I sobbed. "I almost died back there, Aunt Astrid. You don't know. That thing was huge. I mean really huge."

"What thing?"

"The spider." I swallowed hard and tried to tear the tape with my teeth.

"Cath, you've always been known to exaggerate." She stood up and walked to the back of the café, where I'd just come from. "But that's one of the things I love about you."

I watched her go to Bea, who had put the brooms away. I had no idea if she killed the spider, and I wasn't about to go back there and check. Instead, I turned to the customers and smiled sheepishly. "I'm afraid of spiders," I said, finally freeing one hand and pulling the plastic from my head and shoulders.

It could have been during my life-threatening encounter with the arachnid that a striking lady had slipped in. I was positive I would have noticed her. She was wearing a bright-pink shirt with ruffles around the collar and sleeves. Her hair was very blond, almost white, and her eyes were so icy blue that they were almost perfectly clear. At first, she had her back to me, but then she stood, turned around, and took half a step in my direction.

"Spiders aren't bad. They just keep getting judged by the way they look," she said before stepping around me and walking out the door. I didn't see a cup in her hand or a mug left on the table. Had she ordered something? Had she come in with anyone?

I was about to ask Aunt Astrid about it when the bells over the door jingled again, and the sweet smell of barbeque filled the air. Ahh. Lunch was served.

Jake walked in carrying a big white sack. Behind him was Blake Samberg. My hero.

"You didn't get all prettied up for me, did you?" Blake asked, looking down at me with that devastatingly handsome smirk, smelling like cloves and orange spice.

I rolled my eyes at him, trying to smooth out my hair and straighten out my T-shirt. Then I put my hands on my hips.

"There was a spider," I huffed as I continued to try and flatten my hair, which was now standing at attention due to static from my plastic hood. "Where were you ten minutes ago when I was fighting for my life?"

"Picking up your lunch," he replied.

"You're forgiven," I chirped.

He took my hand and pulled me to our usual table for two in the corner by the window, where we shared a lunch of ribs and cheeseburgers.

3

LOOSE ENDS

Blake Samberg was my boyfriend. There. I said it. He'd been Jake's partner at the Wonder Falls Police Department for quite some time. As much as I tried to deny it, I had been crazy about him since day one. But I'm not going to get into all those gory details, because no one wants to know how my knees turned to mush every time I saw him, even when he was being nothing more than a thorn in my side.

As we ate lunch together, he was, as usual, quiet while I prattled on about my near-death experience with the spider that had touched my skin.

"Sounds like your aunt is trying to help you face your fears," Blake said as he wiped his mouth after taking a bite of hamburger.

"Very funny. If that was her goal, it didn't work. In fact, it made it worse," I said with a mouth full of barbeque.

I looked over at Bea, who was helping herself to the ribs on Jake's plate while he sat across from her at the counter, smiling. Quickly, I took out my camera and snapped Bea's picture. After chuckling with Blake, I wrapped up the ribs, unable to eat any more, and told Blake to take them to work in case he got hungry later.

"So, you want to meet me after work?" Blake asked. "Maybe we could take a walk through the park and share an ice cream before I escort you home."

"That sounds nice." I wiped my mouth.

"We've got to work late tonight. That murder-suicide has a couple of loose ends I'm not happy with," Blake said while wiping his hands on a paper napkin.

"Like what?" I asked, not even trying to hide my nosiness.

"Well, how about I save it until I see you later? I think we need to save something to talk about." He smirked.

"What? If you think so. It's okay if we don't have anything to talk about. Quiet is nice sometimes," I added.

"I suppose. But that can be dangerous," he said, his face serious, but his eyes twinkled mischievously. "When you aren't talking, I'm always hoping to kiss you."

My cheeks flashed and ignited, and I just hoped no one was looking at me. Blake gently tucked a few strands of my hair over my ear. He smelled so good. But I was struck dumb and couldn't think of any sarcastic retort. Instead, I giggled like a schoolgirl.

The guys left after lunch, and we got slammed almost immediately afterward with our regular lunch-hour crowd.

That afternoon, on my break, I decided to check out the arts and crafts festival just to stretch my legs.

Silver Valley Park was alive with people at long tables and beneath portable tents, where vendors sold everything from homemade jewelry to pickled beets to recycled paper and any other craft that could be imagined. Local artists featured their paintings, sculptures, carvings, and home décor. It was nice to see so many creative people out there.

The sun was shining, and a pleasant breeze was carrying not just the fresh scent of clean air but also a mixture of the essential oils, perfumes, and lotions some of the folks were selling. It was very relaxing as I strolled with my hands in my pockets, not thinking of anything in particular except seeing Blake and what I was going to make myself for dinner that night. That was the last pleasant thought I had as I suddenly saw the same strange blond woman who had been in the café standing there staring at me. Her icy blue eyes were wide with recognition.

"Hello," she said.

I tried to act casual but was sure I came across looking more as if I'd just walked out of a dark cave, blinking and shrugging and shielding my eyes when no bright light was even shining on me. "Oh, hi," I said.

She was standing behind a long table that was beautifully decorated with lacy doilies and crocheted table runners, with vintage dishes and saucers holding the most wonderful-smelling homemade soaps.

"I hope you haven't encountered any more spiders." The woman was smiling as she stared at me.

I shivered and wasn't sure if it was because of the memory of the spider incident at the café or because of how this loo-loo was looking at me.

"Nope. Forecast for today calls for no spiders." I chuckled and started to walk away.

"We just moved into the neighborhood. Just a few days ago," the woman said. "My name is Cedar Lott."

"We?" I asked hesitantly, not immediately seeing anyone with *Cedar*. Just then, a long, hairy leg pushed past her blond hair, followed by another and another.

I took a step back and bumped into a lady with a stroller.

"I'm so sorry," I said, looking into the woman's annoyed face as she pinched her lips together and nodded at me. When I looked back at Cedar, she was still smiling, not like a crazy jackal or a clown but as if she was watching someone balancing a stack of cups and saucers. There were no hairy legs coming from her hair.

"I have to go," I said. "Your soaps smell wonderful."

"Please, take a business card." She swiped one off the table and handed it to me.

There was nothing out of the ordinary about her fingers. They were pale, the nails unpolished but neat. She wore a large ring on her left ring finger, but I couldn't make out the symbol on it.

Quickly, I snatched the card from her and waved with it as I backed up and walked away. A shiver raced across my shoulders. The sun no longer felt so warm, and I wasn't sure if it was because the canopy of leaves overhead covered me in shadow or if something was following me. Looking quickly over my shoulder, I saw Cedar gazing at me. There was someone behind her, but I didn't want to stare, so all I saw was a shadow of a person. That must have been the "we" she had referred to. How I missed the person I didn't know, but it was a busy festival, and there were lots of people milling around. I must not have kept a good eye on all of them.

Finally, when I was out of view of Cedar's table, I looked down at the business card and stopped in my tracks. It was an image of the pretty Gingerbread House. I cocked my head. This was weird.

"Soap Scents," I muttered as I studied the business card. "Why would they have the Gingerbread House on their business card? They weren't the people who lived there."

I decided to hold on to this information until I saw Blake later in the evening. Maybe it was just a house that looked similar to the Gingerbread House. I tried to think that, but I'd looked at every detail of that place. The dainty shutters and window boxes were all in the same places. The cobblestone sidewalk. The scallops on the roof. Nope, this was the same house. Why was it on Cedar's business card when just this morning, it had still belonged to that newlywed couple? I stuffed the card into my pocket and headed back to work. I'd ask Aunt Astrid what she thought about it.

But as with so many thoughts I had, this one slipped my mind after Blake called and had to cancel our date due to paperwork. Of course, I knew that usually meant there was more to a case than he was ready to admit. And he knew I'd start snooping around if he gave me all the details at once. With his promise to make it up to me, we hung up, and I went back to the café, thinking of him and not Cedar and her strange business card.

❧ 4 ❧

CREEPY GIRL

With the baby coming in a couple more months, Aunt Astrid was more than happy to close the café a little early a couple of times a week in order for Bea to rest and for all of us to help at her house. Today was my day to help in the nursery. Peanut Butter, Bea's cat, bounced all around the room, playing with a Styrofoam peanut that had escaped from a package somewhere.

"Are you looking forward to the new baby?" I asked the kitty as he tossed it up in the air, his tail whipping furiously back and forth.

"Yes, and as soon as I catch this thing, I'm going to curl up against Mom's side and keep him warm in her belly," Peanut Butter replied while knocking the curlicue underneath the changing table only to dart after it.

"Him? Did you say him?" I asked, feeling giddy

inside as I ran my hand from Peanut Butter's head all the way down his back to the end of his tail. He purred but didn't take his eyes off the Styrofoam peanut, which was temporarily out of reach.

"So, what do you think of this color?" Bea asked while munching on a stalk of celery. There was an entire buffet of crudité on the box that held her new changing table.

"That's really pretty," I said as she popped open a can of a lovely soft-yellow paint. "It looks like tapioca pudding."

"That sounds delicious," Bea muttered. "And look at this. Jake is going to paint this all around the trim." She popped open another can of a deep, rich brown.

"This baby is going to be so calm and tranquil in this room. And so is his mama," I said, smiling as I unwrapped a package of tiny bedsheets perfectly sized for the mattress in the crib.

"We don't know if it's a *he*," Bea said.

"Come on. Don't tell me you wouldn't like a little boy running around and screaming *mama, mama* all over the house, tracking in mud and bringing you grasshoppers." I chuckled at the thought.

"As long as the baby is healthy, we're happy," Bea assured me as she rubbed her belly.

"Yeah, yeah. I know." I covered the little mattress as Bea helped herself to a handful of carrot sticks.

"Where would you like this?" I asked, pointing to the little bed.

"There might be a draft by the window. Don't you think it would look nice between the bookshelves?" Bea asked. Jake had purchased two tall bookshelves, because this baby was going to be smart and have tons of books. Coloring books. Comic books. Story books. And I wouldn't have been surprised if Bea had a special spell book for babies to add to the collection.

"I think that will look nice. You just stay where you are, Wide Load," I teased. "I'll move it." As I pulled the crib gently across the room, I looked out the window. Before I could take another step, I froze and then, a split second later, crouched.

"What's the matter?" Bea asked.

"It's that creepy girl from the arts and crafts festival," I hissed, gesturing for Bea to lower herself. Asking a woman who was almost as wide as she was tall to crouch was not a kind or even realistic request.

Instead of crouching, Bea stood on tiptoes from the back of the room to get a look at who I was talking about.

"What are you so scared of? She's probably handing out copies of *The Watchtower*." Bea clicked her tongue and shrugged. "Besides, it looks like she and her travelling companion are moving on. My house looks empty from the sidewalk."

I crawled over to the window and carefully peeked over the sill. Not wanting to take any chances that they'd see me and know we were home, I inched my way up until I saw the tops of their heads. I couldn't miss Cedar's unnaturally natural blond hair. But her friend's had more of a normal hue: a plain brown not much different from mine. It was too risky to get a glimpse of her face.

"Cath, you don't have to hide," Bea said.

"How do you know? If they see us up here, they might come to the door," I hissed.

"So what? It doesn't mean we have to answer." Bea shrugged and took a step toward the window.

"No! Trust me when I tell you there is something strange about that girl and anyone who associates with her." I peeked again. "What the heck? What are they doing?"

"What?" Bea asked and froze before she would have appeared in the window.

Just then, Peanut Butter hopped up onto the windowsill and paced back and forth. *What are we looking at?* he asked.

"They are scribbling on the sidewalk," I replied, peeking between Peanut Butter's legs.

Both women outside were hunched over, each

with a piece of white chalk in her hand. I couldn't see what they were writing, but they were definitely putting something down. I was about to call out to them to knock it off, but before I could, they stood, looked approvingly at each other, and then headed off down the sidewalk.

"They're leaving?" Bea asked.

"Yeah. They're going that way." I pointed to the left.

"Well, I want to see what they wrote on my sidewalk. What if it's a threat or some kind of racial slur?"

"What kind of racial slur could they attribute to us when we're all whiter than white?" I scratched my head.

"I don't know. You know how crazy people are today. Maybe we aren't white enough or we're too white. I don't know. All I do know is that anyone who takes the time to write on the sidewalk in front of a person's house has something serious to say." Bea popped a floret of broccoli into her mouth.

I was on the tips of my toes as we went down the stairs to the front door. Bea, managing her weight as best she could, clomped like an elephant. I motioned for her to stay back as I inched up to the door. There were no suspicious shadows across the beveled glass or hovering back and forth behind the curtains. Still,

I wasn't going to take any chances with my pregnant cousin. I held my finger up in front of my lips, went to the door, and in one swift movement turned the knob and yanked the heavy front door open. A bird chirped from the neighbor's maple tree.

Still, not trusting my own eyes, I leaned out onto the porch and looked to my left and right. "Okay, the coast is clear," I said, waving Bea to my side. I took her hand, and we walked carefully out onto the porch.

"Should we go and look at what they wrote?" she asked.

"Yeah. I guess we better. I'd hate to think there were vulgarities on the sidewalk that the neighbors would be reading," I said, making Bea's eyes widen.

"Who would do that? You don't think they wrote vulgarities, do you?" She put her hand to her lips.

"I don't know."

"That would really be out of line. Jake and I don't do anything vulgar. You and Blake haven't been vulgar, have you?" she asked seriously.

"Well, even if we were, they should be writing in front of my house and not yours," I replied coolly.

Bea looked at me with her mouth hanging open. I squeezed her hand, and we walked out of the house together like we used to when we were kids. It was as natural to hold Bea's hand now as it had been when we were eight years old and heading off to the park with Aunt Astrid just a couple of paces behind us, allowing us our freedom even if it was just pretend freedom. This time, instead of Aunt Astrid, it was Peanut Butter following, his tail high as his eyes spied everything that moved.

"I don't know if I want to see what it is," Bea said, hanging back for a second but never letting go of my hand.

"It'll be okay, Bea," I said.

Finally, we reached the place where Cedar and her friend had been standing and looked at the sidewalk. We saw a pretty design of what looked like a sun with pointy flames around it at the twelve, three, six, and nine positions. There were a leafy-looking thing, a snaky-looking squiggle, three triangles, and an eyeball inside the sun.

"What is it?" Bea asked.

"It looks like something you'd find at the arts and crafts festival that some local talent was selling for way too much money."

"I don't know," Bea said, tilting her head one way and then the other. "I've never seen that before. Do you think it's one of those goofy modern art things that are part of a series? Like a visual scavenger hunt. People have to scour the city to find the markers, and whoever gets them all wins."

"Wins what?" I asked.

"How do I know?" Bea replied.

"Maybe your mom will know what this is," I suggested.

"Even if she doesn't, I think we should tell her about it," Bea said.

I could see she was a little afraid. This didn't sit well with me, either. It was time to tell my aunt about Cedar, the blonde who kept coincidentally popping up everywhere I was.

5

THE SECT OF SYMMETRY

P eanut Butter ran up to the door as a fluffy and stoic Marshmallow watched us approach from her perch in the window.

"Mom!" Bea shouted as she knocked on the door.

"Aunt Astrid! Open the door." I shook the handle, but it was locked. "Is she around back? Maybe she's still at the café?"

"I'm right here," we both heard her shout from inside. "I just thought this was a perfect time for a nap, but I should have known my daughter and niece wouldn't let that happen."

Aunt Astrid opened the door, smirking. She always wore loose-fitting clothes in vibrant colors, and today was no different. Her turquoise dress reached her ankles.

Peanut Butter quickly scooted inside and walked

around the door to hop up with Marshmallow in the afternoon sun.

"Sorry to bother you," I said as I pushed my way past her.

"Mom, something weird just happened," Bea said.

"What? What's the matter?" she asked, putting her hand on Bea's belly.

"No. The baby is fine," Bea said. "No. Something weird just happened outside my house. Ask Cath."

After shutting the door, I slipped the chain into place just in case. We all took seats in the kitchen, where Bea immediately opened the refrigerator and pulled out a jar of dill pickles and some hot giardiniera before grabbing a stack of wheat crackers. I wrinkled my nose at her as I started to tell my aunt about Cedar.

"So, what did this symbol look like?" Aunt Astrid asked. I picked up a pen, and on a piece of scratch paper, I drew the same symbol. My aunt picked it up and studied it for a moment.

"You're sure this is what they drew?" she asked, looking from me to the paper and back to me again.

"Yeah," I replied.

Aunt Astrid walked to her library at the end of the house. It was a beautiful room with a chaise longue and walls covered from floor to ceiling with books on witchcraft, ranging from *The Stupid Person's*

Guide to Spells and Magic to *The Cold-Forged Grimoire*. She came back to the kitchen with a huge book under her arm and my drawing in her hand.

The book she was carrying wasn't a book on spells or even a book on symbols. It was a recorded history of families dating all the way back to Salem, Massachusetts, where our kind didn't originate but, let's face it, were best known.

The book opened with a crackling of the spine. It had that intoxicating smell old books often had, and the pages were extra thin and delicate. We handled them gently with thumb and forefinger alone, one page at a time.

"I know exactly what this is," Aunt Astrid said with a smile on her face. "It's a greeting."

"What? Why not just knock on the door?" Bea inquired after swallowing her third pickle. "I find this a little strange. Why didn't they go to Cath's house? This Cedar person talked with you, right? I don't know who she is."

"What kind of greeting is it?" I shrugged and looked at my aunt.

"This kind. The Sect of Symmetry." Aunt Astrid pointed to the official symbol of this group, which was on one of the delicate, thin pages. It was the same as what had been crudely drawn on the sidewalk in front of Bea's house.

"The Sect of Symmetry?" I asked, shaking my head. That sounded like it had something to do with math and geometry, and I didn't care for the vibe I was getting from it.

"They are very old. I didn't think anyone really practiced this anymore. They aren't like Druids, who are practically extinct. But this was a strict branch of witches, and they had very precise techniques and intense rituals. I often heard stories when I was young about the Sect of Symmetry. They were not the kind of witches you messed with," Aunt Astrid said.

"Name a group of witches you *do* mess with," I said, blowing on my nails and polishing them on my shirt.

Bea chuckled with her mouth full.

"I meant other covens," Aunt Astrid said and winked at me. "If I had to compare them to something, I'd say they were like the Green Berets of the occult world. You had to be a little crazy to be part of it."

"Are they dangerous?" Bea asked.

"I doubt it. I think they are just cautious. You know people like us can never be too careful about who we mingle with."

"How did they know we would be receptive to

them?" I asked. "How did they know we are witches too?"

I had been hoping my aunt would give me a simple explanation that maybe this group had a special sixth sense or even knew about us from their own history or family tree. But she just looked at me and shrugged. That didn't reassure me. Something in the pit of my stomach flipped. There was something about people knowing my business without my consent that felt like a burr under my skin, a pebble in my shoe. I wouldn't die from it, but it was darn annoying.

"Well, I don't know how I feel about them leaving their calling card on the sidewalk. I'm going to ask Jake to hose it off tonight when he gets home. If they want to talk to me, they can ring the doorbell like normal people," Bea huffed as she went back to the fridge and grabbed the milk jug and a tall glass from the cupboard. Just as she filled it, there was a ruckus at the front door.

"You!" I pointed at Bea. "Stay where you are. I'll see what's happening."

Marshmallow and Peanut Butter were suddenly at my side, their hair on end.

"Did you guys hear that?" I asked.

"We were sound asleep on the big couch," Marshmallow said, staring at the door.

I nodded just as there was another thump at the door, as if someone was trying to climb it instead of open it. I squared my shoulders, not sure what I was going to do exactly, but I walked up to the door. I pressed my ear against it and heard quite a bit of cussing and grunting.

"What in the world?" I opened the door to find Jake and Blake both fighting with a large box that had been delivered. "What are you guys doing?"

"Your aunt's rocking chair arrived," Jake said. "We were trying to get it up the stairs. The darn delivery guy left it on the sidewalk."

I walked up to Blake and patted him on the back. "That was sweet of you."

"Hey, I helped too," Jake grumbled as he took one end. Blake, after giving me a kiss on the cheek, took the other.

"Yeah, yeah." I waved him off. "You've got the Queen of Kissy-face waiting for you inside, eating everything in sight."

The guys clumsily brought the box in. My aunt was thrilled. She had ordered the rocker especially for those instances of babysitting when she'd have a new baby with her to spend the night. Peanut Butter instantly perched on top of it while Marshmallow slunk around all four sides before taking a seat next to the box and yawning.

"What are you doing home?" Bea asked, smiling as if she hadn't seen Jake in days.

Blake had followed me back to the counter, where he looked at the book Aunt Astrid had been reading.

"A rough day," Jake replied before kissing Bea as if he'd been away at war.

"What are you doing looking at *The Tome of Progenitors*?" Blake asked.

"How do you know what this book is?" I asked, somewhat annoyed.

"It's important that I learn about your family, your history. It will help me to understand you and where you come from, what you are about."

"You think you can understand me by reading a book?" I asked.

"Maybe a little," he said. I could see by the twinkle in his eye that he was enjoying teasing me.

"Well, I suppose if I was going to read a book to get to know you, it would be something like the dictionary or maybe an old encyclopedia of the letters Q or X," I teased back.

"You stop picking on Blake. You'd be surprised how many hours he's spent here learning about our history," Aunt Astrid said. She always had a soft spot for him. I had to wonder if, in her visions and dreams, she hadn't seen us eventually getting together and that was why she always acted sweet to him.

I rolled my eyes then felt Blake's hand gently rub my back without anyone noticing. Feeling all warm inside, I looked up at him and winked. I'd almost completely forgotten about Cedar and her chalk art on the sidewalk.

"You look tired," Bea said to Jake.

"Yeah, we had another one." He shook his head, loosened his tie, and took a seat on one of the stools in Aunt Astrid's kitchen.

"Another one what?" I asked.

"Domestic dispute. Ended in the death of the woman. Her husband killed himself. We think there might have been drugs involved. If you could have seen the crime scene..." Jake said then looked at Bea and rubbed her belly. "Now's not the time to talk about it."

"Another one?" Aunt Astrid said.

"Yeah. The crazy thing is that it was just down the street from the murder-suicide at your Gingerbread House," Jake added.

"Why does everyone keep calling it *my* Gingerbread House?" I huffed.

"You're the one who liked it," Jake replied. "Even though to me it looks haunted and creepy. Those shutters with the hearts cut out of them and the trim around the roof? It's spooky."

I stared at Jake and shook my head. Then I

snapped my fingers. "I almost forgot." I reached into my back pocket and pulled out the business card for Soap Scents. Without looking at it, I handed it to Blake. "What do you think of this?"

"What am I looking at?" Blake asked. "Soap Scents. Sounds wonderful."

"No, look at the house in the background," I said, pointing at the card but still not looking at it.

"What about it?" Blake asked.

"Look familiar?" I replied.

"No," he said, squinting at the picture.

"It's my Gingerbread House," I said.

"I don't think so," he replied.

I snatched the card out of his hand and took a look. Then I gasped. "Oh, I don't like this one bit," I grumbled. "This was not on here earlier." I stared down to see a business card with the words Soap Scents on it, except instead of the pretty fairy-tale house in the background, there was just a row of soaps. I explained what had been on it before, but it didn't do me any good. No one believed me, and that made me start to doubt myself.

"I think you might have been under a bit of stress after hearing what had happened at the house. You loved that place," Aunt Astrid said.

"Yeah, Cath. It probably shook you up more than you knew," Bea replied. "I should have known to check on you. You are so much more sensitive than you let on."

"No, I'm really not," I argued. "But I swear I saw that house. It seemed so real."

"Of course it did. But now that you've had time to relax and the shock has left you, you're seeing clearly. It's just the natural progression of things," Aunt Astrid added. "You poor thing. How about a cup of tea?"

I accepted my aunt's tea, but I wasn't convinced I had been in shock when I'd first received this business card. There was something strange about Cedar and her friend, and none of it sat well with me. Just because they knew some ancient greeting didn't mean they could be trusted.

I kept this to myself, but when I looked up at Blake, I could tell he knew what I was thinking. I was thankful for that.

6

MEMORY LANE

Much to my chagrin, Bea did not have Jake hose the chalk off the sidewalk like she'd said she was going to. When I came out of my house the next morning, I walked across the street to Bea's place. I'd promised to escort her to the café while she was in her wobbly stage.

"How did you sleep?" I asked her as she opened the door to greet me.

"Pretty good. Lots of kicking last night." She patted her tummy.

"That's probably from the pickles and giardiniera you ate at Aunt Astrid's," I teased. I looked her up and down and shook my head. "You know, I don't get it. How is it that all that extra tonnage in the front can still make you look like a prom queen? Meanwhile, here I am after a homemade oatmeal facial, a banana smoothie for breakfast, and egg-white conditioner freshly washed out of my hair, and I look like I just got off my shift at the truck stop."

"Oh, stop it," Bea said after pulling the front door shut. She linked her arm through mine as we walked down the sidewalk together. "It's baby glow. Besides, you aren't fooling me, Cath."

"What?" I asked, pinching my eyebrows together.

"You've had that *I'm in love* glow on your face every day since you and Blake finally set your differences aside and admitted you're lost without one another." Bea huffed and looked straight ahead, avoiding my narrow gaze.

"Have you been drinking? Bea, it's not good for the baby," I snapped back.

"You can't fool me, Cath." She squeezed my arm. "You and Blake are a perfect fit. He's straitlaced and you're..."

"Careful, Wide Load," I teased.

"And you are the fabulous, amazing *you*," she replied.

"Hey, why didn't you have Jake hose off that chalk in front of your house?" I asked.

"I didn't think there was any reason after we all talked yesterday. I didn't want to seem rude. After all, it was a greeting. If I had erased it, they might have thought that I was saying for them to just go bugger off. Why?" Bea shrugged.

"Don't you get the feeling it's a little weird?" I asked.

"Yeah. But then again, I think if they are witches, it isn't unusual for them to be weird," Bea replied.

I couldn't argue; she had a point there. But when we arrived at the café, I wasn't just thinking the Sect of Symmetry was weird. I was beginning to think it was dangerous. At the end of the block, I was sure I saw Cedar's long white-blond hair along with the taller, brooding friend she'd had with her outside Bea's house. They were walking away, but Cedar turned quickly, and I knew she saw Bea and me. Bea was almost impossible to miss with her red hair and big belly. And who else would be with her but me?

When we stepped inside the café, it was still dark. Kevin was in the kitchen, but even his normal rattling of pots and pans seemed subdued.

"You feel that?" I asked Bea, who nodded. It felt like a funeral parlor might after a child had died: heavy and sad and dark.

"Mom?" Bea shouted and pushed past me toward the back of the café. I grabbed Bea's arm and pushed ahead of her. If there were going to be any shocks, I was going to keep her back and see them first.

"Kevin?" I yelled. He quickly peeked his head out of the kitchen.

"What? Is everything okay?" He looked oblivious to any trouble.

"Where's my mom?" Bea asked.

"Uh, I saw her go in her little nook to do one of her palm readings or whatever it is she does in there," Kevin replied. "Is she all right?"

"I'm all right." My aunt came out of the little cubby where she read tarot cards and tea leaves. Her eyes were red with tears, but she was smiling.

"Mom! What's wrong?" Bea asked nervously.

I was not as concerned with my aunt as I was with the people I'd seen walking away from the café. Bea wasn't picking up on everything. She probably had her wires a little crossed due to the baby. I knew if I was feeling "a disturbance in the Force," it had to be strong, since that wasn't my specialty. I looked at Aunt Astrid. Bea took one hand and I took the other and helped her to her favorite seat at the end of the counter.

"Nothing is wrong. Nothing at all. I had a couple of visitors." She looked up at me. "Cedar and her sister, Ethel."

"What did they want?" I grumbled.

"Cath, always so suspicious." Aunt Astrid

chuckled and smoothed my hair. "They wanted to talk. They were afraid to come to us because—"

"Because I wasn't all that friendly to them?" I said.

"Well, yeah. But they also weren't sure if we'd reciprocate. The Sect of Symmetry is not like us. Well, they aren't all that different. We all practice witchcraft, but some people just do it a little differently, maybe are a little more intense than we are." Aunt Astrid chuckled.

"Why are you crying?" Bea asked, still worried about her mother.

"They did a past reading of me." Aunt Astrid chuckled again and sniffled at the same time. "No one has been able to do that for me in ages. You have no idea how much of my life I've forgotten. Some of it from age but some of it I'd put out of my mind."

"Like what?" I asked. This didn't sound right to me. Who from any branch of witchcraft busts into a person's place of business to give them a free reading into their past lives for *no reason*?

"Oh, things that happened so long ago. My life before you." She touched Bea's chin. "When your mother and I were young women together before we settled down and had our families," she said to me. "There's so much I had forgotten."

"And what was the point of this stroll down memory lane?" I huffed.

"Well, I think they were just being nice. I think it was Cedar and Ethel's way of making introductions. We witches have to stick together." My aunt smiled as if she was not only trying to convince me but maybe also herself that there was nothing to this.

"Mike Warner's mother was a witch. Don't try and tell me we need to stick together," I snapped.

The thought had barely formed in my head before it spilled out of my mouth. My ex-boyfriend's mother had had many amazing talents and had used them all for evil as if it was a sport.

"Leave it to you, Cath, to see the negative first," Aunt Astrid said, laughing and shaking her head. "Funny. Cedar and Ethel said you would. But they still invited you to the barbeque."

"What barbeque?" Bea's eyes lit up. She was totally thinking with her stomach.

"Cedar and Ethel and their family are having a barbeque, and they have invited us to join them," Aunt Astrid said cheerfully.

"I'm not going," I said.

"When is it?" Bea asked, looking from me to her mother and back again.

"This Saturday," Aunt Astrid said.

"I gotta work that day. I hope they understand

that we have a business to run." I walked behind the counter, grabbed an apron, and proceeded to wrap it around my waist.

"Cath, don't be silly," Aunt Astrid said. "We are running in the black and have been for a long time. We can afford to close early one day."

"I thought we were saving that closing-early day for Bea's big day," I said.

"We can do both," Aunt Astrid said, patting Bea on the arm before diving into her receipts. "Bea, honey, go ahead and unlock the door. Cath, better get that coffee brewing. Bea, your tea, please. And could you make your mom a cup of the honey-mint?"

"Sure, Mom." Bea looked at me. She didn't like the idea of taking any extra time off when she had a little bundle on the way. Plus, it was not like her mom to just close the café for what was nothing more than a picnic with some people we barely knew.

I didn't say anything more about it the rest of the day. Bea didn't need stress around her. And my aunt looked as if she was getting back to her old self just as quitting time came around.

By the time I was in my house, the doors and windows securely locked and the air-conditioning humming quietly, I didn't know what to think.

7

FAST-FORWARD

Treacle peeked at me from outside the kitchen window. When I walked into the kitchen, I heard the meow and saw the green eyes looking at me.

"Nice of you to come home," I said as I slid the window open.

"There are some strange things going on in the world," Treacle said as he slunk across the windowsill and hopped onto the counter, sitting patiently as I closed the window and went to get his dinner ready.

"Why do you say that?" I asked as I pulled down a plate and reached into the cabinet for a fresh can of cat food. "Just because there have been two strange murders on the same block, one of them in *my* Gingerbread House, and a couple of weird women chatting up Aunt Astrid doesn't necessarily mean there are strange things going on."

"*Funny you bring up the Gingerbread House,*" Treacle said as he watched me scooping his food onto the saucer. "*While I was out, I watched an anthill grow to twice its size in the yard of that house.*" He licked his paw.

"That sounds gross. What do you mean it grew?" I asked.

"*It was like the ants were on fast-forward.*" Treacle stood, turned to face me and his saucer of food, and slowly began to eat. "*I know ants are busy all the time, but it was like something had prodded them to move even faster, so the anthill grew even faster. Do you understand what I mean?*"

I shook my head and shrugged. "You watched this happen?"

"*I was mesmerized,*" Treacle replied as he licked his chops. "*I stayed there until I heard the sounds. Then I didn't want to stay any longer.*"

"What sound?"

"*Clicking and a screech like a barn owl.*" Treacle then gracefully slid his front paws down the cabinet below the counter before hopping down to the floor to rub around my legs as his way of saying thanks for dinner.

"Interesting. What do you say we stay in tonight and watch an old movie and forget about the strangeness happening outside?" I pulled the freezer door open. "I've got some homemade chicken soup I can defrost. That sounds good. There isn't anything that chicken soup can't make better."

"I'll meet you on your bed." Treacle purred and hopped up, making himself comfortable on my pillows while I popped the soup into the microwave and proceeded to get undressed, wash my face, and put on my jammies. By the time I found a good movie to watch, the soup was defrosted and ready. I put it in a mug, turned the AC a few degrees cooler, and pretended it was Christmastime in July.

Treacle and I watched some crazy Marx Brothers movie. I wasn't sure which one, but I laughed nonetheless. Then there was a Montgomery Clift movie on that I'd never seen before, and when it ended, there was some gangster film I had never heard of. When I looked at the clock, it was a few minutes past eleven. I yawned and scratched Treacle, who was completely zonked and stretched out on the left side of my bed.

I took my soup mug to the kitchen and double-checked that I'd locked the front door. When I peeked through the curtains, I didn't see anything out there that looked out of the ordinary. At least, not in front of my house. But just as I was about to let the drapes fall back into place, I saw two figures standing on the sidewalk in front of Bea's house. And it was that all-too-familiar blond hair hanging down that made me pinch my lips together.

Part of me wanted to go out there and ask what the heck they were doing. But another part of me said I was outnumbered and maybe outgunned. So I slipped into stealth mode and grabbed my phone while I shut off the lights and dialed Bea's number.

"What's up, coz?" Bea answered.

"Is Jake home?" I didn't want to alarm her right off the bat.

"Yes, he's here. Why?" Bea asked, but then I heard her talking. "He said to tell you to give your lips a break. Blake had to stay at the station. He had a lead on something and was going to follow up."

"Let me talk to Jake," I said quickly.

"I'm sure Blake will call you," Bea said. "You know how cops are."

"I do. And I'm sure he will. That's why I would like to talk to Jake for a minute." I was about to start yelling, and then the snoopers outside would probably hear me.

Finally, Jake took the phone from Bea. "Cath, he's at work. All he does all day is sit quieter than usual with a look of sheer happiness on his face since you guys got together. He'll call when he's done and—" Jake teased before I could cut him off.

"Jake, I didn't want to alarm Bea," I whispered

loudly. "But there are two women standing outside your house staring at the place. They are the ones who drew that symbol on your sidewalk."

"Really?" Jake instantly became Detective Jake Johnson.

"Yeah. It might be nothing. But I just thought it was something you should know." I let out a deep breath. "If you want me to go and shoo them away, I will."

"That won't be necessary, Cath. Thanks, though. I'll take it from here," he said.

"Okay. Call if you need backup."

I didn't hear Jake chuckle as I'd expected him to. I had worried him. But it was better to let him know what was happening than to worry Bea while she was in her delicate condition. And there wasn't anything Jake wouldn't stop with his bare hands, if necessary, to protect her and the baby. I thought I had made the right decision in calling him.

"Thanks, Cath. You too." Then there was a click.

I watched as the lights in Bea's house started to go off. The porch lights came on bright and strong, as did the backyard floodlights. No one was going to ambush them, that was for sure. I went to the kitchen for a glass of water. When I returned, the women were no longer in view. They had either left, vanished, or been abducted up and away into the mother ship. Still, I double-checked my doors and windows.

When I finally climbed into bed, I looked at Treacle.

"Wake me up if you sense anything," I said as I snuggled beneath the blankets.

"Of course," he replied. He remained on the pillow opposite my head, his head raised majestically as his eyes narrowed to green slits.

Even though he was napping, Treacle—or any cat —was better than a home alarm system. Especially when the intruder might have the ability to walk right through the walls. And I was afraid Cedar and Ethel might have that very power. I shivered and wished I hadn't turned the AC up so high.

8

HAIR

My eyes popped open when the sun was just starting to rise. Treacle had moved, stretched out as if he'd been on a bender and had just made it to the foot of the bed before passing out. I scratched his belly before I got up and hit the shower. The previous night's excitement had dulled slightly after a good sleep. I was sure that if anything had happened at Bea's place, Jake would have called, or I would have heard the police cars that would have rushed to the scene.

When I stepped outside, the air was already warm. The smells of dew and sunshine filled my nose, and I thought it was a beautiful morning. I'm usually not that cheery in the morning, so I should have known something would go wrong.

Treacle slipped out the door before I pulled it

shut and headed off into the bushes, where he disappeared.

With the house locked, I skipped down the sidewalk in the direction of Bea's house. But before I made it across the street, I heard wild laughing and chatting as if a party had just cleared out. My heart stopped and lodged in my throat as I saw Cedar, Ethel, and Aunt Astrid coming out onto her porch.

I stood in the middle of the street, watching. None of them noticed me. Before any of them could look in my direction, I pulled my feet from the spot they'd stuck in and hurried to Bea's front porch. It was like being in high school and trying to hide from a group of mean girls who were shopping at the same store when I was out with my mother. I pressed my back flat against the siding of the house next to the front door. When it opened and Bea stepped out, I quickly shushed her with my index finger in front of my lips.

"Why?" she whispered.

"Those Moonies are at your mom's house. They just came out the front door," I replied as Bea carefully peeked in the direction of her mom's house.

"That's weird," Bea whispered. "I think they are leaving."

"Are they coming this way?" I asked, my eyes wide.

"No. It looks like they are heading the other way," Bea said, waving me forward.

"If we get to the café and they've opened the place up, I'm going to have a coronary," I said as I joined Bea and we slowly walked to Aunt Astrid's house. "There is something just plain wrong about those women."

"If they are witches, that's probably true. We shouldn't judge a book by its cover," Bea said as she waddled next to me as we made our way up Aunt Astrid's sidewalk.

"What do you know? These days, you'll follow anyone who promises you a burrito and a bowl of salsa," I teased while I scanned the front porch of my aunt's home for any unusual drawings, trinkets, or symbols. As far as I could see, the coast was clear.

Bea went up the steps first, took hold of the door-knob, gave it a twist, and nearly smashed her face against the glass.

"What the heck is this locked for?" She banged on the door, annoyed. When Aunt Astrid opened the door, Bea and I stood and stared.

"Hi, girls," she said as if there was nothing wrong.

"M-Mom? What did you do to your hair?" Bea stuttered. Her long hair had been cut.

"Oh, don't fuss," Aunt Astrid said. "I had been

wanting a change, and this isn't even that big a change."

"Mom, about five inches of your hair is missing. It just barely falls over your shoulders," Bea said. "It's just a shock is all."

I looked past my aunt into her house for the trimmings to indicate where she'd gotten her hair cut. I didn't see anything. I didn't see Marshmallow, either.

"Excuse me. Too much coffee this morning. I like it, Aunt Astrid. I bet you feel lighter," I babbled as I skirted past her into the house.

If I were to tell the truth, I'd have gently told my aunt, who had been the only woman in my life who could come close to my own mother, that whoever had cut her hair had taken lessons from a third grader. But I was more interested in finding where all her hair had gone. There were so many reasons this was bad that I hardly knew where to start.

I dashed upstairs into the bathroom and saw not a single stray hair on the floor or in the small trash can. I went from room to room, hoping I might find a circle of hair on the floor, but no luck. As I eased back downstairs, I quickly hurried around the staircase to the library, the downstairs bedroom and bathroom, through the kitchen, and finally around the front-room furniture and still didn't see a single strand. In the kitchen, I peeked into the trash, but nothing was there either except a few spent tea bags. Three teacups sat in the sink.

Finally, I saw Marshmallow, and she was sitting patiently on the back deck, staring into the house through the sliding glass door.

"*What happened to you?*" I asked her.

"*That's what I'd like to know. One minute I was warm and cozy, the next I was wrapped in a sickly-smelling arm and being tossed outside,*" Marshmallow replied.

"*What did they put you out for?*"

"*Probably because they knew I would have scratched their arms off had they laid a hand on my person. There is something wrong with those people. And they left a horrible stench in the house. Do you smell it?*" Marshmallow sneezed.

"*I don't. But I believe you.*" I stroked Marshmallow's fur. "*Stay close to her, and if anyone else comes to the house and they put you out, come to the café.*"

"*Ugh, it's bad enough the house smells, but now I might have to venture out of doors like a common alley cat.*" She stretched.

"*All right. Go to Peanut Butter. Stay close to him,*" I replied and got a deep purr in response.

"Aunt Astrid, what happened to your hair?" I asked innocently, pointing to the floor as I stood up, leaving Marshmallow to find a place to sit and listen.

"I got it cut. Just a trim. Please explain to my

daughter that it's no big deal," she said, rubbing her eyes. "I just thought it might be fun."

"I think it looks fine. Especially if you like it," I soothed. "But where are the strands? The hair that was cut off—where did it go?"

"Oh, Cedar and Ethel must have cleaned up," Aunt Astrid said casually. "Now, before you girls go off half-cocked, Cedar and Ethel asked if you could each bring a side dish to the barbeque. I said of course you could. They left some of their soaps here. Would you like some? They don't smell too bad."

Now it was getting serious. It was one thing for Aunt Astrid to do things like let strangers into her house or let them cut her hair, but it was another to offer my culinary talents to people I didn't know and who didn't know me. And when I say culinary talents, I mean I have none. Cheez Whiz on saltines. Pretzels poured in a bowl. Those are what I call party sides.

Bea looked at me as I snapped my mouth shut and grimaced. "Don't worry, Cath. I'll make something for both of us," Bea said before I could utter a single squawk. "Come on, Cath. Let's open the café. We'll meet you there, Mom."

"Oh, I might be in late. Cedar and Ethel were here so early. I might lie down for forty winks," she said as she not-so-subtly pushed us out the door. "See you later."

I was about to protest when the door shut in my face. I whirled around to face Bea, my mouth hanging open as if my jaw had been snapped and my eyes bugging out of my head.

"This is weird," Bea whispered as she took my hand and we walked off the porch and headed to work.

"Weird. There isn't a single strand of her hair in the house. They took it. You know what that means?" I hissed.

"No." Bea squeezed my hand.

"Well, it means that they are a couple of freaks who convince older people to let them cut their hair and then they collect it," I huffed. "There has to be a reason they took it. We need to look in your mom's library. As much as I hate to say it... we need to do some *research,* and we need to do it without her knowing what we're doing."

"Why can't we tell her?" Bea asked, her forehead wrinkled with worry. "If she's in trouble, shouldn't we tell her?"

"She doesn't seem to be all that worried. Cedar and Ethel have convinced her they are normal and just looking to build a support group of witches," I huffed.

"Maybe that's all they are?" Bea said without much conviction in her voice.

I looked at her as I pulled the key from my pocket and slipped it into the lock on the front door of the café. "Then why are they skulking around at the corner, staring at us?" I said as I nodded toward the end of the block.

Standing there, just staring at us, were Ethel and Cedar, her icy blond hair blowing slightly in the breeze and her icy eyes staring at us.

9

PILLSBURY DOUGHBOY

The day of the barbeque, I watched the hours tick by one minute at a time. Attending was the last thing I wanted to do, and I felt like we were all willingly walking into some kind of trap. Aunt Astrid had given me a bar of the soap Cedar had made. I didn't think it smelled good at all. It was sickly, as if it had been made with rotten meat or baked garbage with a squirt of cheap air freshener over it. I tossed it soon after Aunt Astrid gave it to me and didn't think twice about it.

Blake had called me earlier to wish me luck at their barbecue.

"I don't want to do this," I mumbled over the phone.

"I know you don't. Your personality doesn't lend

itself to this kind of situation," he said bluntly. "You aren't a social butterfly."

"No. I'm not," I grunted.

"But one good thing about that is that you have that gift of blending into the background. A real wall-flower," Blake said.

"You really know how to make a girl feel confident!" I snapped.

"That's exactly what makes a good detective: someone who can be present but not really noticed," he said. "There are very few who have that ability. You do, at least when you aren't speaking."

I smiled despite my annoyance. "I think that was some kind of compliment."

"It was." He cleared his throat.

"How are things coming with the murder-suicides? Any groundbreaking discoveries?" I asked, changing the subject as I rubbed my blushing cheeks.

"Funny, but no. In fact, Jake and I were just discussing the total absence of groundbreaking discoveries. Like the scenes had been scrubbed. Which is strange, since both deaths occurred in the homes. And the instant sale of the Gingerbread House was also very strange, since it—"

"What? It sold again already?" I huffed. If that didn't add insult to injury. "It's only been a couple of days."

"I know. I find it odd. But there have been stranger occurrences in Wonder Falls than that," Blake said. "Just the other day, a man who had been reported missing more than two months ago was found. He'd decided he wanted to live off the grid and did so by utilizing the city's sewer systems. He'd come up underneath the stores, where he proceeded to steal what supplies he needed. The human mind can adapt to any situation if the desire is there. Uh oh."

"What's wrong?"

"We've got a call. I have to go. See you tonight?" Blake asked.

"Sure. I'll tell you all about my horribly awkward and uncomfortable time at the barbeque." I rolled my eyes.

"Just remember, be yourself. Blend in. You'll find out more that way," he encouraged before hanging up the phone.

I hung up too and sat there for a while. It was almost time to go meet Bea. She was driving. The Gingerbread House was only about fifteen minutes away at a casual stroll. That meant that with Bea driving, it would take at least a half hour, maybe longer, to get there.

When I'd asked her if Aunt Astrid was coming with us, she'd said no; Cedar and Ethel had arranged to have her picked up. That was another thing I didn't like. We all live within walking distance of each other and yet they wanted to only pick up Aunt Astrid? Rude.

Earlier, I had asked Treacle for a favor.

"You know where the Gingerbread House is, right? The one with the anthill?" I said as I stroked Treacle's fur.

"Yes," he said while purring.

"I want you to go there and get a look at things. Tell me what's going on when I arrive. If there is anything shady or strange or unusual. I'll meet up with you later."

"I can do that," he said, stretching as I opened the kitchen window for him to slink outside.

"Stay out of sight. For all we know, that brand of witches eats cats," I said before I slid the window shut and locked it behind him.

That had been about two hours ago. Finally, I heard Bea honk the horn out front. I grabbed my party side dish, smoothed out the front of my T-shirt and jeans, and headed out the door.

"You look nice," Bea said. Her belly was nearly touching the steering wheel.

"Thanks. So do you. Do you want me to drive, or are you teaching the baby to do it?" I said as I pulled the door closed.

"I know. I can't believe I've still got a couple months to go. You'll have to roll me down the street.

What is that?" She eyeballed the plastic party tray covered with tinfoil.

"We had to bring a party side dish," I replied.

"I told you I'd bring something for the both of us," Bea said.

"What are you trying to say?" I asked as she pulled out of my driveway and headed in the direction of the party.

"Well, you aren't known for your culinary talents," Bea said sadly. "I just didn't think you'd want to make anything."

"That I wouldn't want to or couldn't?" I asked, lifting my chin.

"Come on, Cath. You know you can't cook."

"Sort of like how you can't drive? Come on, Granny. The speed limit is our friend. No need to stay so far back from it."

"Very funny. Safe driving is no accident." Bea smirked.

I chuckled when she laughed, and we ended up laughing together. That was until I realized where we were heading. I had walked down this road a dozen times and driven down it more than that, all to pass by the Gingerbread House and try and get a glimpse in the windows.

"Wait a minute. What's the address of this shindig?" I asked.

"It looks like it is that house right there," Bea said slowly. "Oh, Cath. They bought your Gingerbread House."

"But it only just recently became vacant. The murder-suicide, remember?" I huffed.

"I do remember," Bea added.

"We're talking a matter of days. How did that happen? I'm suspicious already. I don't think these witches deserve my party side dish," I grumbled as we pulled up in front of the house. I saw a couple more cars in the driveway.

"At least we aren't the first ones here," Bea said.

My guts tightened up as Bea and I walked to the door. She was talking quietly to me, but I wasn't sure about what. I was sure I was going to have a panic attack, because I didn't want to be here, and I knew that Bea, who was always much more sociable than me, would attract conversation like butterflies to a flower. Meanwhile, I'd be somewhere off by myself counting ceiling tiles or cobblestones.

Without hesitating, Bea opened the door and walked right in.

"Is that proper to just walk right in?" I asked.

"I don't know. I have to go to the bathroom again." Bea rolled her eyes.

"Okay." I looked around. It was like the set of a bad 1960s horror film: lots of red and black fabric and drapery and tacky pentagrams and black candles were scattered around. It was such a beautiful little cottage that I couldn't believe the horrible way it had been arranged on the inside, as if a group of high school kids from the drama department had decorated the place for their senior Halloween party.

"Is this for real?" I muttered.

"I don't know, but I see a powder room over there," Bea said and left my side to waddle to the bathroom.

I stood by myself for a second, my party plate in my hands. Finally, a woman who looked like the Pillsbury Doughboy in a flowery summer dress came up to me. She smiled with lips that were thin and slightly discolored, pushing the corners of her mouth deep into her cheeks.

"Hello! Let me guess. You must be Cath," she said while extending a plump hand toward me.

I held the tray in one hand and accepted her greeting with a nervous smile. "Hi," I muttered. "My cousin Bea is here too. She's in the bathroom."

"I'm Luann. Welcome to our little coven." She giggled. "Let me take that from you. Come on in, and I'll make all the introductions. Of course, you'll already know your Aunt Astrid. She's out in the back-yard with Cedar and Ethel."

"I'll bet she is." I couldn't help saying it.

"What?" Luann asked, blinking her tiny eyes.

"Nothing." I forced a smile that I knew crinkled my eyes and shrugged. *When in Rome* was all I could think. "There's Bea." I let out an audible sigh of relief as she came hobbling in our direction.

I made a quick introduction and then made an excuse to hang back a little. "I have to pee too." The words rolled out of my mouth so elegantly.

"Sure. Well, you know where it is. Bea, let's get you and your little bundle something to eat. When are you due? Is it a boy or a girl? Do you have any other children?" Luann wasn't shy with the prodding.

I went into the powder room and waited an appropriate amount of time before leaving. There was a red candle burning on the edge of the sink with a homemade label on it that read Dragon's Blood. How original. It did smell nice. I was alone in the bathroom just enough time to look through the cabinet beneath the sink. It was filled from top to bottom with nothing but toilet paper.

"I knew they were full of it," I said.

Finally, I opened the door and peeked around. Everyone had gone outside. With the house relatively empty, I thought I'd go exploring. A staircase led to what I could only imagine were the bedrooms. Along the wall were black-framed portraits of sinister-looking men and women from the Victorian era.

High collars and stiff-shouldered jackets adorned the males and females, who had been forever immortalized by the wet-plate photo process from back then.

And yes, their eyes did seem to follow me as I walked up the steps.

10

LITTLE SKULL

Thankfully, the rooms upstairs were not as tacky as the living room downstairs. I couldn't imagine that whoever owned the place could have unpacked everything. I didn't see any boxes or storage bins anywhere. The first room I looked in was horrifying. It held a plain bed with a faded white bedspread and a woven area rug beneath it. The dresser had a round mirror attached to it. The window had Irish lace curtains hanging in front of it. Sure, it doesn't sound scary, I know. But add an ancient ventriloquist dummy, sitting on the bed looking right at me with one eye missing, and the whole image becomes a horror.

Without lingering, I walked down the hallway to the next room. It was also very plain. Nothing stood out as particularly scary, but it seemed very out of character for the rest of the house. It was so pretty outside that every time I passed by, it felt like it was welcoming me, urging me to come sit on the porch, enjoy a cup of hot cocoa or ice-cold lemonade. Instead, these tacky people gave the house the feeling of a hooker in a funeral parlor.

The bathroom looked like it was under some kind of construction. Tiles were chipped off the walls. There was a bucket in the bathtub. The shower curtain was torn. The faucets might have been elegant and beautiful at one time but now were old and coated with calcium. There were several utility buckets filled with the soaps they were pedaling at the arts and craft show in Silver Valley Park. Did they even make that stuff, or did they just buy a bunch of cheap, gross-smelling soap and sell it to people?

The real shame was that this house was adorable from the outside. When it went up for sale, I'd thought it was probably just as cute inside as it was outside. I knew an old couple had sold it to the newlyweds before moving to Florida. Now the newly-weds were dead, and the place that was obviously a fixer-upper wasn't being fixed up.

It made me sad and a little angry. What was with this coven that they'd cheapen the appearance of a nice little home? Didn't they want to live here in

Wonder Falls for at least a couple of years? Why else buy a house?

At the end of the hallway was one last door. The crystal doorknob sat above a long keyhole. I gave the knob a slow turn, but it was locked. So I did what any guest in someone else's house would do: I dropped to one knee and peeked through the keyhole. It was darker inside the room. I detected a hint of a musty smell, as if the room hadn't been aired out in a while. It might have been just a room to hold old furniture, books, clothes, and blankets. I assumed it was nothing more than a storage room until I heard something shift inside.

Something was moving. Maybe it was a mouse. Maybe a squirrel or raccoon had gotten inside and had made its home somewhere among the boxes and furniture. I leaned closer to the keyhole, squinting to try and see something inside. I put both hands against the wooden door to support myself as I strained to see what was in there. But as I looked down for a second to inch even closer, I gasped. From underneath the door, two long, bony fingers were quietly and insidiously stretching and scratching toward my foot.

Without thinking, I fell backward, kicking my legs as if those two gray digits could somehow detach themselves from whatever they were attached to and scurry up my leg—or worse, drag me through that tiny slit beneath the door. From behind the door, I could hear someone or something breathing, grunting, and I was struck with a terrifying thought that whatever was attached to those fingers was looking right at me. Terror shook me by my shoulders as I got to my feet and hurried back toward the stairs. I held my breath as I stopped myself at the top of the flight for fear someone might see me come barreling down like a bat out of hell.

With the tingling feeling of eyes on me, I refused to turn around. If I did, I knew I'd see red or yellow glowing eyes staring back at me from the crack beneath the door. Instead, I casually walked down the steps as if I'd been at the house a thousand times. I looked at the wonderful woodwork that would have been so pretty had the walls been painted a soft yellow or some other happy color. Instead, the room was coated with neglect and accented with vulgar, stereotypical trinkets. And if that wasn't bad enough, I saw something that I would never forget. As I made my way to the kitchen to go out to the backyard, where my family had been ushered, I saw a skeleton... of a cat.

"What in the world?" I mumbled as I looked closely at the sad little skull and delicate, needle-like claws. "What kind of witch would keep a skeleton of our most trusted familiar?"

My question was answered as soon as I looked to the left of the bones. The Sect of Symmetry coat of arms depicted a crone strangling a cat in one hand while holding a statue of the inverted triangle that is supposed to symbolize the Earth.

I decided I didn't want to be scared of this group. I was angry and annoyed. There was something wrong with the whole place. And when I walked into the kitchen, I was in for another shock.

This part of the house was up to snuff with high-end appliances. It boasted beautiful cabinetry and a huge marble counter covered with fresh fruit, veggies, and sweets of all sorts. I could smell cookies baking, and they smelled just about done. But the scent of cookies and the fresh fruit didn't appeal to me. In fact, all the combined scents made me feel like I had motion sickness. My stomach folded over itself, and a rising in my throat made me worry I was going to make a scene. I needed some fresh air, and I needed it fast.

"Hello there. You must be Cath." I heard a scratchy female voice from across the room.

I looked up to see an older lady chewing on what looked like a vanilla bean staring at me. Now, if I was going to listen to little kids describe what a witch looked like, it would strongly resemble this woman. She had gray hair piled on her head in a bun. One eye was bigger than the other and bulged slightly from the socket. She had a long, hooked nose. Her skin was dotted with liver spots, and while she wasn't stirring a caldron, she was stirring something in a crockpot.

"Yeah." I forced a grin but was keenly aware that my stomach needed a cool drink of water and some fresh air.

"I'm Hannah. Everyone is waiting for you outside." She nodded with a sugary sweet grin and went back to chewing on her vanilla bean.

I managed to mutter a thank-you and quickly went outside. If I felt like that after just meandering through the house, I could only imagine what Bea was feeling. With her senses so highly tuned, she had to be lying down somewhere, if she hadn't passed out altogether.

Quickly, I opened the sliding back door and stepped out into the fresh air. Almost immediately, my head cleared and my stomach settled. And there was Bea, with a heaping plate of fruit, standing next to Luann, smiling, and patting her belly happily.

"There you are," she said when she saw me appear. "I thought I'd lost you." She quickly slipped her arm through mine and squeezed.

"You know I'm never far behind. Not with our little guy in the oven. Someone's got to make sure you're eating right for him," I joked innocently as my head cleared and my stomach settled down.

"Him? Are you having a boy? I thought you said you didn't know the sex of the baby yet," Luann snapped, her smile tight, her eyes intense.

"We don't. Cath is just hoping that if she refers to the baby enough as 'him,' it will be a boy." Bea chuckled. I didn't like how Luann was looking at us and especially at Bea's belly.

"You can't change destiny. You might be destined to have a girl," Luann pushed.

"I hope not. Girls can be so high maintenance," I replied with my own sugary-sweet smile. "Besides, we've got enough estrogen to go around. A little testosterone would be a pleasant change."

"Oh, Cath. Come on. You know we just want the baby to be healthy," Bea said.

"You're right. I want the baby to be healthy," I replied as I looked around the yard. There had to be a cooler around with some bottled water or something cold to drink in it.

Luann gave one of those quick, fake smiles and excused herself to go into the house.

"Where is your mom?" I whispered. "We gotta get out of here."

"Why?" Bea asked and bit into a slice of watermelon.

"If you saw what I saw upstairs in this place, you wouldn't be asking me." I quickly described the scene and mentioned the gawdy, stereotypical décor in the front room when we walked in.

"Sure, they are weird," Bea said.

"Bea, didn't you hear me? There is something locked away in the bedroom upstairs that has long, bony fingers that tried to touch me from underneath the door. I'm going to have nightmares for weeks," I protested in harsh whispers. "Plus, they have the skeleton of a cat in their front room."

"What?" Bea swallowed hard.

"Yeah. And I don't think these people are just an innocent clique looking for some kind of sorceress support group. I think they want something from us."

I finally spotted my aunt. She was the center of attention, standing with Cedar, Ethel, and two other ladies I hadn't met yet. Luann had rushed over to a mailbox of a woman wearing a skort and a huge, baggy T-shirt; she had given up on concealing her ample bosom. They looked at me while they talked.

"I think you might be right," Bea said.

"What was Luann asking you about?" I said, trying to look as if I was having a decent time. I tugged at the hem of my T-shirt, looked at the card table in the corner of the yard that was covered with snacks, and saw my plate right in the middle of everything. I tugged Bea in that direction so we could walk and talk without being too obvious about wanting to leave.

"She was just asking about the baby," Bea replied, but within seconds of saying those words, she frowned. "In fact, she wanted to know a good bit about the baby. And our history of delivering children. And when Jake's birthday was and if we needed a midwife, because Ethel is a midwife."

"Ew. They offered midwife services when you just met." I shivered. "I've known you my whole life, Bea. I love you like a sister. But there would be no way I'd want to see south of the border, especially with a baby coming, if I could help it. I think I'm going to pass out from the thought of it." I swallowed hard.

"Pull yourself together." Bea squeezed my hand. "So, what do we do?"

"Let's just act natural for now. We need to get your mom to leave with us. I don't think it would be wise to leave her alone with these ladies." I smiled as I looked around the yard.

There were strange sculptures and lawn ornaments scattered around. The sun was starting to set, and before I knew it, there was a nice fire burning in the pit in the center of the yard. Had these women not been so weird, this would have been a nice place to hang out. They even had a "she-shed" that I watched my aunt go into with Cedar.

"Bea, why don't you sit down and finish your fruit? I'm going to go and get your mom. She hasn't spoken with us all night."

Bea did as she was told, and I walked across the yard in the direction of the shed.

"Hi, Cath!" Suddenly my route was cut off by Ethel. I'd never heard her speak before. Her high, feminine voice didn't fit her slouchy form.

"Hi. Ethel, right?"

"Yes. Are you enjoying the barbeque?" she asked.

She was rather plain in comparison to Cedar, whose clear eyes alone were enough to leave a mark in a person's memory. Ethel had dull brown eyes and mousy hair that hung down to her shoulders. There was nothing about her features that stood out in particular except that she had very long natural nails. They were the prettiest and most feminine thing about her other than her voice.

"Yeah. But I don't think I've actually tasted any barbeque," I said, looking around.

"It hasn't been brought out yet. The coals aren't hot enough." She nearly cracked her face as she grinned awkwardly.

"Oh well, no worries. I'm just going to see my aunt. I haven't said hello to her yet, since you and Cedar picked her up. Normally she travels with family." I took a step and was again cut off by Ethel, who managed to stay in my way.

"Yes, well, I think she's talking with Cedar," Ethel replied.

"I know she is. They went into your she-shed" I pointed. "So, it was nice chatting with you. I'm sure we'll talk again."

"Tell me, Cath, how long have you and Detective Samberg known each other?" Ethel asked innocently enough.

"Who told you I was seeing Detective Samberg?" I asked.

"Your aunt had mentioned it," Ethel replied, her dull eyes suddenly alive with a spark of anger behind them.

"That's personal. I don't care to talk about my relationship." I tried to take another step, but Ethel was not to be deterred.

"That's a dangerous job. I bet you worry a lot." She swallowed hard and leaned in toward me. "I've heard the suicide rate is high among those in law enforcement."

My blood ran cold. Who talked like this? Was this woman trying to tell me something, or was she just a thousand times more socially awkward than I was? I had gone off at a funeral once about the Texas Body Ranch where, in the name of science, they study the decomposition of dead humans in a gigantic field. The daughter of the deceased had not been impressed. And to add insult to injury, if I remember right, I told her that her lovely, deceased mother was probably too old to be studied for very long. Nice, I know. Awkward: that was me.

"I don't think the suicide rate of our police force is a proper topic of conversation here," I snapped. "If you'll excuse me."

I literally had to push past Ethel, using my arms and elbows to get her out of my way. As soon as I did, I saw my aunt appear in the doorway of the she-shed. She was smiling and laughing and barely noticed me.

"Aunt Astrid?" I called.

"Oh hi, Cath." She smiled. Behind her, I saw Cedar, who glared at Ethel and then me.

"What were you looking at in there?" I asked.

"Hi, Cath. I was just showing your Aunt Astrid some of the trinkets I've collected over the years. So, tell me, how is Blake Samberg doing?" Cedar asked smoothly. "Your aunt was just telling me about you two."

I looked at my aunt, unable to stop my eyebrows from pinching in the middle. Of all the people on the planet, she knew how private I was. To have my business being shared with people who were nothing but strangers to me was not just embarrassing but aggravating.

"I hope you don't mind, honey. I was just bragging on you and told them about you and Blake finally finding one another," Aunt Astrid said as if she'd told them nothing more than that I had brown hair and worked at the café.

I was about to grab my aunt by her arm and drag her out of the house when I heard my name being called.

"I'm in the bushes to your right!" Treacle called. *"Don't eat the barbeque!"*

"I think the barbeque is almost ready!" Luann shouted from across the yard, where she was standing by a black barrel smoker. The other guests clapped and shouted. The smell seemed heavenly at first, but I detected a sickly odor underneath it.

"Don't eat it! Don't eat anything they cooked!" Treacle shouted.

"Why not?"

"They've done something to it. It isn't good meat," he replied.

I carefully looked around and spotted his green eyes peering at me from beneath a thick bush. Treacle was nothing more than a shadow to anyone else who might be looking around. His black coat was perfect camouflage, and I was glad he was staying out of sight. Especially after having seen the cat skeleton.

"Stay where you are," I ordered.

"Trust me. I'm not going anywhere. These women are not like us. Not at all," Treacle said.

When I looked back at Aunt Astrid, she was not paying any attention to me but rather was chatting with Cedar, who was watching my reaction.

"Aunt Astrid, did you say hi to Bea?" I asked.

"Oh, I will. Just give me a minute," my aunt said as she slowly started to walk away with Cedar.

Ethel bumped me as if to urge me in the opposite direction of the she-shed. I obliged and hurried over to my cousin, who looked at me with wide, worried eyes.

"What happened? The look on your face was like nothing I'd ever seen before. Did my mom do something?" she asked, her left hand resting on her belly. I gave her a quick replay and watched as her eyes widened with surprise.

"That's not like Mom at all," she said before sniffing the air. "That barbeque smells good. I'm starving."

"No. Don't eat it," I warned.

"Look, if nothing else, I'm getting a free meal out of these witches," Bea argued.

"I mean it. Treacle saw something and said don't

eat anything they cooked. You haven't, right? You just had some fruit. Hopefully there wasn't anything on that," I mumbled.

"Cath, I hear what you're saying, but there is something about that smell. I can't not eat it. I want to. I *have* to," Bea said.

"Look, Jake will be happy to get you barbeque again. Heck, I'll drive to Ronny's on 5th Street and pick you up a bucket of ribs and some chicken too. Just promise me you won't eat anything here. Please?" I looked toward the bushes, where Treacle was waiting for me.

"What's wrong with the meat? What did you see?" I asked, shouting in my head.

"I don't think it's an animal like a cow or a pig. Not from what I saw. And these women did a ritual over the spices. Just don't eat it," Treacle begged.

"I can't help myself, Cath. I'm starving and—"

"Treacle says he doesn't think they cooked beef or pork," I hissed, holding on to Bea's hand. "Bea, can't you sense my nerves? Can't you sense how worried I am?"

She looked at me and then at my hand touching hers. Her eyes widened, and just then, we both felt the baby kick.

"I don't feel anything," she mumbled. "Cath, what's wrong with me?"

"It's not you, Bea. It's this place. Let's get you out of here," I said, quickly getting to my feet and putting out both hands to help my cousin up. It took two tries.

"Should we say good-bye?" she asked.

"No. You need to think about the baby, not your manners," I said as I quickly walked her toward the sliding glass door. But just as we were about to slip inside the house, Ethel and Hannah casually blocked our route.

"Cath?"

"Come on. Hold my hand and pretend you are studying the architecture and the lawn ornaments," I said as I led her around the perimeter of the house. The backyard was enclosed by a privacy fence, but there was a gate at the side of the house. I'd seen it on several of my visits to admire the house from afar. We pretended to chat casually, but Bea choked on more than one occasion as she pointed out the weird lawn décor that she said she'd seen in some of her mom's books.

"Good," I said. "Get in your car and go straight to your mother's house. See if you can find those in any of her books. Maybe we can figure out what it is we are really dealing with."

"Can I stop at Ronny's on the way first?" She blinked at me.

"I think so. As long as you promise to go right home after that. You both do have to eat." I squeezed her hand as I looked around the yard. There wasn't anyone paying any attention to us. Quickly, I opened the gate, and Bea wobbled as fast as she could to the car. I stood and watched until she was safely behind the wheel and pulling out onto the street. In typical Bea fashion, she *slowly* drove away.

I let out a sigh of relief until I turned around to find Hannah glaring at me, her eye bugging even more.

"My cousin wasn't feeling good, so I told her to go home. With the baby and all, I didn't want her to take any—"

Without any warning, she took hold of the gate and pulled it shut, leaving me alone in the front yard.

Treacle was still in there, but I knew he could escape over the top if he had to. Aunt Astrid would have a much harder time. I had to get back in there before she ate anything.

I dashed to the front of the house and walked right in the front door. Still, no one was in the garish front room. Without waiting, I hurried through the house, fighting off the nausea that seized me again. When I reached the sliding glass door, I tugged it open just in time to see my aunt take a bite of something from the barbeque pit. My heart sank to my feet.

Everyone seemed to be watching her eat. No one noticed me and instead kept smiling and talking and enjoying passing out the strange food they were determined to make everyone eat.

Aunt Astrid was talking about how good everything tasted, how pleasant the place was, and how disappointed she was in Bea and me for leaving the party.

"They might be a little jealous, Astrid," Cedar said. "We understand you a lot better than they do. We see that often in families of witches, where some members become downright nasty if another member really starts to excel and understand their powers."

Just as Ethel was scanning the yard, I slipped behind a thick bush that stretched across the length of the fence. Treacle quickly came trotting up to me.

"This isn't good." Treacle looked intently at me.

"Tell me about it. We're stuck behind a shrub watching Aunt Astrid eat some kind of bad food and forget all about us," I replied. *"Did you hear that Cedar person? Who does she think she is getting in between family? Someone ought to punch her in the face."*

"Easy now," Treacle soothed.

"This isn't right. This isn't just a coven of witches. This is a cult. They've got some kind of agenda, and somehow

Aunt Astrid has become the object of their desire," I thought. "I gotta just go get her and drag her out of here."

"No. Don't. There isn't anything saying they'll let you go. You are outnumbered. By a lot. Just wait. This shindig can't go on forever."

Treacle was right. So we hunkered down for the long haul and watched as Aunt Astrid talked and laughed and hugged and held hands with half the guests in attendance. But it wasn't long before she was yawning and claiming to be tired.

"This was a wonderful party," Aunt Astrid said.

"Well, you are welcome any time. We have lots of fun and would love for you to join us," Cedar said. "In fact, we want to officially invite you and Bea to join our family."

"What? What about me?" I thought, looking at Treacle.

"That's so kind of you," Aunt Astrid said. "We witches do need to stick together."

"I'm a witch. How come she isn't asking about me?" I clenched my teeth.

"Because that isn't your aunt. They've done something to her," Treacle said.

"You can say that again," I replied.

More comments passed among the mutual adoration league before my aunt made it to the front door to leave. The entire coven escorted her out, and once again, Cedar was my aunt's chaperone, making sure she got home without dealing with Bea or me in the process.

Before Treacle and I were able to slip from our hiding place, Hannah appeared again and began to scarf down some of the barbeque that was still on the grill. I didn't know if there were any bones in what she was devouring, but the way she stretched her mouth open to eat, it wouldn't have made a difference. She tore into the meat with no concern for bones at all.

"Ready?" I looked at Treacle.

"If you are," he replied.

"Just follow me."

I squared my shoulders, stood straight, and, as if there was nothing more natural than coming out from behind a row of bushes, emerged from my hiding place. I looked directly at Hannah, who looked directly at me. She didn't move. I nodded, turned, grabbed hold of the latch of the gate, and fumbled with it as my hands shook. I was sure I heard heavy footsteps quickly coming up behind me. If I turned to look, there would be Hannah, her eyes almost out of their sockets as she glared at me, her hands stretched out to take hold of me and dig through my shirt to pierce my skin.

So I didn't look behind me. Instead, I focused on

the latch. Treacle scaled one side of the fence, and I heard his paws softly pad their way down the other side. I swallowed hard, focused, and finally got the latch open. I dashed out and pulled the gate closed behind me. Within seconds of Treacle and I getting out and dashing across the dark lawn of the neighbor's house, the gate flew open, and I was sure it had gotten ripped from its hinges.

"That was a close one," I said breathlessly as Treacle and I began to make our way to Aunt Astrid's house. It would take us about half an hour on foot. That was okay. I didn't mind the cool night air, which was fresher out on the street than it had been in Cedar and Ethel's crazy gingerbread fun house.

12

RATS IN THE ALLEYS

Had I known Treacle was going to lead me through back alleys, patches of forest, and two subdivisions to get home, I would have stayed at the Gingerbread House and eaten the barbeque. There were rats in the alleys, I walked through three spiderwebs in the forest, and... well, nothing happened in the subdivisions except that I saw a bunch of fancy houses. But we did get to our street in twenty minutes instead of thirty. My house looked normal. Bea's was unusually dark, and my Aunt Astrid's was not only well lit, but Cedar was still chatting her up at the front door.

"Stay out of sight," I instructed Treacle. He left my side to slink closer to the house on his own, completely undetected.

I, on the other hand, had to be a bit more careful.

I carefully ducked from shadow to shadow as I inched closer to my aunt's front porch. Thankfully, it was elevated above the rest of the yard. But I still had to cross the neighbor's yard. I dropped to my hands and knees and crawled across the grass along the bushes that lined the front of their house. The grass was cold and wet, and I was sure that I touched a worm and maybe an anthill. The crickets were chirping, and a few bright stars were twinkling in the beautiful dark-blue sky. The moon was just a sliver, glowing brightly and adding another beautiful shape to the night sky. It was hard to look up at the peaceful sight and then realize I had to get to my own aunt's house by sneaking along the ground.

"It will be the greatest move you've made," I heard Cedar say in a low voice.

If they convinced my aunt to sell her house, I was going to scream.

"I don't know what my girls will think," Aunt Astrid replied.

"You have to explain things to them like children," Cedar said. "They'll probably protest at first until they see what you've gained."

I crawled through the cool, wet grass in the dark another ten feet until I reached the porch and pressed my back against the siding. Cedar's voice was low but firm, as if she was giving my aunt orders. No one gave Aunt Astrid orders. Who did this woman think she was?

"I agree. But what if they don't want to join me?" Aunt Astrid's voice sounded tired.

"You just need to bring Bea along. Cath isn't your child. You are only related to her through your deceased sister."

Again, I felt my insides tighten. I wasn't just some stranger. Aunt Astrid loved me like she did Bea. She had told me that a million times, and I'd never doubted her. If it was the last thing I ever did, I was going to punch this Cedar woman in the mouth.

"Cath might come if Bea does," Aunt Astrid added.

"It doesn't matter. If you want to invite her, you can. It's always good to have a few extra numbers in case an extra body is needed. But remember, Astrid, this is really about you. You've been floating around without any direction. No real connection to the life of witchcraft and those who practice. It's time we come out from the shadows, spread our message. And if people won't accept us, well, they'll end up like the people who lived in our house."

The Gingerbread House? A murder-suicide? What had Cedar and the rest of them had to do with that poor newlywed couple?

"We just need to acquire two more homes. One is

already just awaiting signatures. Then the last one, the one you'll live in, it will complete the pattern, and there will be no stopping us," Cedar continued.

"It's a lot to think about, Cedar," Aunt Astrid said with a yawn.

"We don't have a lot of time. A decision must be made," Cedar pushed.

I wanted to march up the steps and tell her to get off the porch, but I remained still.

"I'll know tomorrow. I think it's all that food. I need to rest," Aunt Astrid said.

"But you can tell me now," Cedar continued. "That way I can report back to the rest of the coven whether or not we are ready to proceed."

"I can't. I need to rest and talk with Bea," Aunt Astrid said.

That reminded me: Where was Bea? I'd sent her home to find Aunt Astrid's book and match the stuff we had seen in the yard to descriptions in Aunt Astrid's book. That would be like finding a needle in a haystack.

"Fine! Rest! But Ethel and I will be back tomorrow morning when the sun comes up. You had better have a decision for us!" Cedar barked.

"Please don't be mad," Aunt Astrid begged.

This wasn't like her at all. She was normally like a duck letting water roll down its back when it came to people's opinion of her. Why was she worried if this blond bimbo was mad at her? She wasn't even related to her like I was. She was technically *nobody*.

"I'm just putting you on notice, Astrid, that this is not an invitation that should be taken lightly," Cedar said. "Okay, so you said you were tired. And I said Ethel and I will be here in the morning. You'll see when you wake up that we're offering you an amazing opportunity. Now, let me give you a sleeping spell so you'll sleep well tonight."

A sleeping spell? I listened to Cedar rattle off words in a language that didn't even sound real. There was no Latin, no Greek, nothing that I even remotely understood. Now, of course, I wasn't the most astute student, and I had probably forgotten most of my spell lessons from when I was a teenager. But this was a low, guttural language, and I didn't like it. It sounded sinister.

"Now go to bed. Make sure you answer the door tomorrow morning." Cedar huffed and stormed off the porch as if my aunt had stolen her bicycle. I watched her get in her car and drive away before I dashed up the porch steps and burst into the house. Thankfully, Bea was there, standing over her mother. Astrid had collapsed on the couch, already asleep.

"Did you hear all that?" I asked Bea. She nodded. "What do you make of it?"

"I think they've done something to my mother," she replied with tears in her eyes.

"There's no time to cry, Bea. We have to find out what it was she said to your mom. I'll bet it's in one of Aunt Astrid's books."

I started to go to the library but stopped.

"She put a sleeping spell on her. But, if I heard her right, it wasn't for a deep or peaceful sleep. It was to keep her mind restless." Bea sniffed and wiped her nose on the back of her hand.

"Why in the world would anyone do that?" I asked.

"I don't know. That might be in one of Mom's books," Bea said. "Cath, she's so pale. She looks exhausted."

"Marshmallow, where are you?"

The big Maine coon came suspiciously down the hallway. She'd obviously been in the spare bedroom.

"I wasn't going to risk that woman seeing me," the big cat said. *"She gives off a horrible smell. And I think she's passed it along."* Marshmallow padded up to Aunt Astrid and carefully sniffed at her. *"Yuck. It's a sick smell, like something is dying or rotten."*

I was glad Bea couldn't hear what Marshmallow was saying. "Can you do anything to help her while I search the books for something that might undo this spell?" I asked.

At the sliding door, I heard Treacle meow. That was exactly what we needed. I hurried over and opened the door.

"They must have all left the party when Aunt Astrid did," he purred. *"I just saw them all taking turns driving past."*

"What? All of them? That's crazy." I then asked Bea, "Is Peanut Butter here or at your house?"

"No. He's all alone. Jake and Blake are working on those murders. They won't be home until late," Bea gasped. "I'll go get him."

"No way. You two stay here with your Aunt Astrid," I said to the cats. "I'll go get him."

"Be careful. They are obviously keeping an eye out for someone. If I had to guess, I'd say it was you," Treacle said.

I nodded, slapped off the outside lights, and told Bea to lock the door behind me. I slipped out the sliding back door and crept around the house.

Sure enough, there was a strange car parked at one end of the block and another parked at the other end. I stuck to the shadows as I had when I snuck up on my aunt's house. I alternately crawled on my belly and ran from one patch of darkness to another and made it to Bea's front porch unnoticed. I wasn't sure why I was shaking. I didn't know what these people had against me. I had never done anything to them except think they were weird. Maybe they could all read minds and were offended by that. If that was the case, then they should have known I was here. But not a single car moved.

Peanut Butter appeared in the window, looking at me with surprise on his face.

"I'm going to crack the door. When I do, run to Marsh-mallow's."

"Are we in trouble?" he asked through the glass.

"Yup," I replied.

"Is it the people who have been walking up and down the street?"

"What people have been walking up and down the street?" I asked as my heart started to race. I could taste the dryness in my mouth.

"Those people," he meowed, looking down the street.

Just then I saw Luann and Hannah stomping in my direction. Quickly, I opened the door, slipped inside, and quietly shut the door behind me. I snapped the dead bolt and slipped the chain into place. I put my finger up to my lips and looked at Peanut Butter, who remained in the window.

Luann and Hannah came up the porch steps and looked around as if they'd lost a contact lens or maybe an earring, feeling their way all over the porch. When Hannah looked at the window, she hissed at Peanut Butter, slapping a thick, meaty hand hard against the glass and making the poor kitty jump and meow. He hopped down and came to my side.

"*What's wrong with them?*"

"*They don't like cats,*" I replied. "*And that says a mouthful about them.*"

They searched and slunk around a little while longer. Then I watched through the peephole as they went back down the steps, down the sidewalk, and to the end of the block, where they stood and stared.

"*So, what do we do?*" Peanut Butter asked.

"*You ready to run?*"

"*Sure.*"

It wasn't the greatest plan, but I thought the element of surprise might be enough.

"*Okay. When I open this door, you just take off for Aunt Astrid's place. Don't worry about me; I'll be right behind you. Go up on the roof if you have to. Bea will hear you and let you in.*"

"*I won't leave you by yourself with those cat haters.*"

"*Don't worry. I'll handle them if I have to.*" I wasn't sure what I actually meant by that, but it sounded good and tough and put Peanut Butter's mind at ease. That was the most important thing right now.

On the count of three, I opened the door. Peanut Butter did as he was told and took off like a bullet in the direction of my aunt's house. I slipped out and pulled the door shut behind me. I swear I made eye contact with Luann, who pointed at me like Donald Sutherland at the end of the remake of *Invasion of the Body Snatchers*. Her eyes went wide, and her mouth fell open in a silent scream. My blood ran cold. I took off running for my aunt's house. Although I am not the most athletic person—in fact, I hate exercise of any kind—I did sprint like an Olympic gold medal winner across the neighbor's uneven yard and up my aunt's front porch, taking two steps at a time before hurling myself against the door.

"Let me in! Bea, let me in!"

I looked over my shoulder, and sure enough, that cockeyed Hannah was pumping her legs as if I had stolen her purse. It would have been a hilarious sight, since she was wearing a strange black skirt with black tights underneath. But her face had transformed from plain ugly into a mask of hatred.

Before I could start screaming, the door opened, and I literally fell inside. As I pulled my legs up, Bea slammed the door shut and slipped the lock into place. I got to my feet and dashed upstairs to find Peanut Butter perched outside the front bedroom window, licking his paw.

"What took you so long?" he asked.

"Very funny. Get downstairs with the rest of them," I ordered.

"That woman is scary. Wait until I tell Marshmallow

how she pounded the window at me," Peanut Butter said as he came inside the house and trotted toward the door.

I followed him back downstairs and went to Bea's side.

"What was that all about?" she huffed. "Who was that chasing you?"

"Oh, that was just cockeyed Hannah. Yeah. She was at the barbeque. One eye is bigger than the other. You didn't see her? I don't know how you missed her. Yeah. She was staking out your house. And mine, too, I guess. Yeah. She was chasing me."

"Chasing you? What for?" Bea gasped.

"I don't know. I guess she doesn't like me very much. None of the people in this coven do. They keep talking about Aunt Astrid and you, but I'm like the black sheep." I scratched my head. "I can't quite figure it out."

"She's probably jealous," Bea said. "Is she still out there?"

I peeked out the window, and a shiver ran across my shoulder blades. "It isn't just her. Luann, Ethel, and that blue-eyed witch Cedar are all standing on the sidewalk as well, two to the north and two to the south, staring at the house."

"What?" Bea put her hand to her throat and walked to the window. "Oh my gosh! They're like picketers. What are people going to think? They're going to think that my mother has groupies or something. This is horrible."

"Hey, as long as they are out there and we are in here, it's not so bad." I patted Bea's shoulder. "How is she?" I pointed to my aunt, who was asleep on the couch. Despite all the noise and hubbub, she didn't move a muscle.

"I guess she's okay. Sleeping. But she keeps grumbling and fussing like a baby with the flu. It's hard for me to watch," Bea said. "I don't think she's going to be much help."

"No. We need to find out about that spell that Cedar put on her and also about the symbols and carvings of things at the house. Plus, I'd also like to find out what kind of witches kill cats," I said, unaware my teeth were clenched.

"Witches that kill cats?" Marshmallow asked, but all the cats looked up at me.

"That's right. We're dealing with a couple of real *ladies,"* I huffed as I walked to the library. "I want you guys to hold a vigil for Aunt Astrid until I tell you to stop. Hopefully, it won't take us long to discover what they did to her."

"Will she be all right?" Treacle asked as he took his spot to the right of Aunt Astrid and Peanut Butter took the left. Marshmallow sat at my aunt's head.

"Yes. She's going to be fine," I said. "So long as everyone does their part. You guys hold the fort. We'll be in the library. Anything happens, call me. Don't leave her alone for a second," I ordered, getting three simultaneous meows in response.

Bea and I scoured the library. It wasn't until the sun started to come up that we thought we might have an answer to Aunt Astrid's ailment. But just as we emerged from the library, Aunt Astrid woke up.

At least, it looked like Aunt Astrid.

13

SUSPICIOUS OF EVERYONE

My aunt had been taking care of me since I was a kid. I had known my mother, and I knew what had happened to her: a literal monster under the bed took hold of her and dragged her under there with it while I watched, screaming. I had been too young to help but too old to pretend what I'd seen was some kind of bad dream or fairy story to cover the hurt of being an orphan.

My Aunt Astrid would never be my mother. Not because I didn't love her; I loved her like crazy. But there had been something about my mom, something about her eyes and her perfume, that was specifically hers that could never be fully replaced. I had never thought my aunt felt slighted because I didn't call her Mom. She wasn't my mom. She was my beloved aunt who had raised me to embrace my gifts and remember that the name Greenstone was a name to be proud of.

So when Bea and I saw her start to stir from her place on the couch, sit up, and blink, we let out a sigh of relief.

But when she licked her lips, scratched her head, and then stared straight ahead with terror creeping into her eyes, we immediately knew something was wrong. Of course it was. Those witches had done something to her last night. Her mouth fell open in a silent scream.

"Mom? Mom, are you all right?" Bea hurried to her mother's side and took hold of both her hands.

I quickly gathered the cats, and we hurried to my aunt, who was beginning to cry.

"Aunt Astrid, what's wrong?" I asked.

Bea held her mother's hands tightly. "Cath, she's in trouble," Bea whispered.

Holding her hand, Bea told me she could not just sense but could see that her mother's aura was flashing like a Christmas tree. Something terrifying had seized hold of her.

"Aunt Astrid, can you see us? We're right here. What's the matter?" I got down on my knees in front of her with the cats all around me.

"Bea? Cath? I can't see the other dimensions anymore," Aunt Astrid gasped. "I can see you both without your beautiful auras, without the past and future overlapping. It looks so desolate. Everything looks dead to me."

"What?" Bea muttered.

"It's all gone. Everything is gone!" Aunt Astrid tried to stand up, but the shock of what she was seeing—or wasn't seeing—made her go pale and nearly fall over. "It's all so lifeless and lonely. How do you stand it? How can you stand looking at a life like this?"

"Mom, it's going to be all right. I'll make you some tea and—" Bea offered.

"Tea? What in the world good will tea do?" Aunt Astrid barked.

"All right, Aunt Astrid, you need to calm down and calm down now." I stood up. "I'll tell you what happened. You ate the food from the cauldron of those witches, who are really strangers, down the street, and they put the whammy on you."

"Don't you talk about them that way," Aunt Astrid whined. "They are my friends. Do you know how long it's been since I talked to women my own age? Women who truly understand me?"

"Cedar isn't your age. She's *my* age at most," I griped. "And you are going to have a cup of tea and calm down."

I looked up at Bea, who stared at her mother like she would an unruly child.

Aunt Astrid shook her head. "You wouldn't understand. Cedar has an old soul," Aunt Astrid blubbered.

"Mother, you need to sit still and take a couple breaths. You are hyperventilating," Bea said as she watched her mother's face get red and her eyes bug.

"I've got to go talk to them. They'll help me. They won't criticize and judge me." Aunt Astrid wasn't even talking like herself. If there was one thing my aunt was not prone to, it was pity parties. I didn't like this look on her one bit.

"Aunt Astrid, you aren't going anywhere until Bea makes you a cup of tea. Bea, please make your mother a cup of that special tea."

Bea nodded and stomped into the kitchen, where she quickly put on the kettle and grabbed a few special tea leaves for her mother's condition.

"They told me you were going to be a problem. They said that you were going to find fault with them and not want to let me go." My aunt looked at me suspiciously.

"Oh, did they?" I chortled. "Well, considering I'm family and you raised me, I guess they aren't keen on your parenting skills. You made me love you as if you were my own mom. Boy, you suck at parenting."

I rolled my eyes and hurried Bea along with the

tea. My aunt was fussing, and the way she was looking around, I was sure she was trying to figure out a way to get past me and run out the door. But I could tell her new vision, or lack thereof, was causing her serious problems, because she was so used to maneuvering through a couple dimensions at least that she was probably blinded by simplicity.

"I don't like your smart remarks, Cath," Aunt Astrid replied.

"Well, take a number," I replied and took the steaming cup from Bea. "Drink this. You'll feel better afterward."

"Thank you, Bea," my aunt said as she took the cup. "This is just horrible. I feel like I'm looking into a desert. Everything is so plain and empty."

"Don't worry, Mom. It's probably just temporary," Bea soothed. "Do you remember anything that might have led to this? Anything from last night? It was late when you got home, and Cedar brought you. Did she say or do anything that might have caused this?"

"No," Aunt Astrid snapped. "And you sound just like Cath. Suspicious of everyone."

"It's a gift," I replied as I walked to the front window and peeked out. As I scanned the street, I couldn't say I was surprised to see Cedar and that big behemoth, Ethel, lumbering along with her toward

Aunt Astrid's house. I looked over my shoulder at Bea.

"This tea is good, Bea, but it isn't bringing my visions back," Aunt Astrid whined.

"I didn't think it would," Bea stuttered.

"Then what did you give it to me for?" Aunt Astrid said as she took another sip. Her attitude was like that of a spoiled child.

"To calm your nerves... way down," Bea said and looked at me.

As soon as she did, I saw my aunt's eyelids get heavy. She raised her hand to speak and pinched her eyebrows together in an angry scowl but fell back asleep before she could utter a syllable.

"How long do we have?" I asked.

"A couple of hours. Cath, what are we going to do? Did they steal her gift?" Bea looked ready to cry.

"All right, *you* calm down," I said. "That baby needs his mama thinking happy thoughts. Besides, we've got company." I jerked my thumb at the door just as we both heard footsteps on the porch.

"So, what do we do?" Bea rubbed her hands together.

"Cover your mom with that blanket and the pillows on the couch. Then go to the library," I snapped. The last thing I wanted was to be worrying about Bea and her baby. I knew in the library she'd have access to whatever she needed to protect herself. It was like a Green Beret running into his gun closet.

That left just me to face them alone. It was strange. I had faced multitentacled monsters, black-eyed kids, a giant rat, and a mud-man, just to name a few things off the top of my head. I must have earned my sea legs, because this band of misfits didn't scare me. Maybe it was because the sun was shining. Maybe it was because I knew Bea and the cats were with me.

Maybe I'd finally lost my mind and didn't see danger the same way anymore. That was probably it.

14

THE COOL CLUB

There came a pounding on the door as if the fire department was about to kick it down. It was a rude, abrasive knock, and I didn't like how I got the sense they expected my aunt to jump and run to the door and let them in.

I had had about enough of these witches. With Bea in her condition and Aunt Astrid in hers, it was like we were driving a car with the air quickly running out of the tires. But I had a trick up my sleeve. Quickly, I grabbed the table salt and poured just enough to cross the threshold of the door. Then I yanked the door open, making Cedar and Ethel jump before they could have a chance to knock again. They made an attempt to step inside, but the salt was just enough to stop them. And boy, did it make them mad.

"What are you two witches doing here at this hour?" I scolded. "It's not even time to get up for work yet."

"What are you doing here?" Cedar asked through clenched teeth.

I folded my arms across my chest and shifted from my right foot to my left. Cedar looked over my shoulder and saw Aunt Astrid lying on the couch and pointed at her.

"She needs our help. Sweep aside this salt and let us in," Cedar said, squinting at me with anger. Ethel was no better. Like a coiled snake, she was just waiting to spring at me. Suddenly, I heard all three cats hissing and growling. At the windows were the other witches, glaring in at all of us, and I swear that Hannah was actually drooling.

"You set one foot inside this house and I'll bite it off." It was the first thing that came to my mind. Part of me hoped she wouldn't call my bluff, but as I heard my favorite familiars cheering me on from behind, another part of me sort of hoped she would. I squared my shoulders and stood my ground.

"You're going to cause more harm than you know," Cedar replied, peering over my shoulder for a look at Aunt Astrid. "Neither your aunt nor your cousin should be anywhere around you."

"Now, that's just rude. I don't know why I'm not

cool enough to be in your club," I huffed. "I mean, judging by your clubhouse back there, which looks like Aleister Crowley decorated it, you are hardly the kind of people who should be throwing stones."

"We aren't here to talk to *you*," Cedar hissed. "We want to talk to your aunt."

"Sorry. She's not seeing guests or annoying throwback witches from the Puritan era. Why don't you all hop on your brooms and head on back to Salem," I snapped back.

"You think you're very funny, don't you?" Ethel grumbled.

"I've been told as much," I replied. "Now, you're on private property. Unless you want me to call the police and have you removed, I suggest you head on back home to make sure no one dropped a house on anyone in your coven."

"You'll be sorry," Ethel said. Cedar stood stone-still with her arms at her sides, glaring at me. "When we've got all the pieces in place, you'll crawl on your belly for our protection. You and those filthy animals will be fed to the serpents, and you'll feel the burning of your own—"

I shut the door and ran to the library. The cats quickly followed, but I ordered them to stay with my aunt.

"She needs your protection now. Maybe especially

now that she's actually asleep and resting, whether she likes it or not," I instructed the felines before giving them each a rub on their heads. "Keep her safe, and yell if you need me."

Just as I tried to enter the room, I was knocked back by an invisible force that sent me flying backward into the wall. I bumped my head.

"Oh! I thought just in case they got you," Bea apologized. She rattled off a couple words I didn't understand as my head spun slightly.

"No. That was smart," I said as I rubbed my head with one hand and waved my other hand past the doorframe to make sure Bea had removed the spell.

"What did they want?" Bea asked as she flipped through the thick book she'd been holding when I tried to walk into the room.

"Your mom," I said. "There has got to be something in here that can help us. Hey, what was that book your mom said she found that symbol in that they drew outside your house?"

"That was *The Tome of Progenitors,*" Bea said.

"I'm going to start there. Maybe there is something about that family crest that will help us figure out what they are really all about."

I went back into the living room, because that was where I had last seen the book when Blake was talking about it as if it was the latest on the *New York*

Times Best Seller list. I looked at the cats, who were all sitting protectively around Aunt Astrid, their eyes narrow slits as they saw and heard everything without moving a muscle.

After checking every flat surface and coming up empty-handed, I started scouring the shelves to see if my aunt had put the book on a shelf, out of the way. I was quite surprised when I kicked it as I scooted past the couch.

"Why did she leave it on the floor?" I asked the cats as I held it in my arms and flipped it open. "It's not like Aunt Astrid to be so careless."

"It wasn't her," Marshmallow purred. *"I can tell by the markings all over it."*

"Ew. Let me guess. Was it one of the Sect of Squares who hid it here?" I held the book out to Marshmallow as if it were contaminated. She purred a yes.

"Why would they hide her book?" I thought. *"Unless there was something in it they wanted to hide. And they probably didn't have enough time or the ability to just walk out of the house with it. Maybe that's why they came back and were so desperate tonight."*

"I don't know. But I was hiding under the couch when they shoved it under there," Marshmallow replied before narrowing her eyes again. I looked at the big cat and shook my head.

"And why were you under there? That had to be terribly cramped for you."

"The smell. They all give off that bad smell. Sick and pungent," Marshmallow said.

I just nodded and took the book back to the library. There had to be something in it, that was true. But it contained more than five hundred pages. I flopped down next to Bea, and we began our research.

I went to the pages on the Sect of Symmetry and began reading. At first it was as boring and uninformative as Cedar and her group were. But then something jumped out at me. It was the symbol of greeting they used, the one they had put in chalk in front of Bea's house.

"Bea, is this the same design as in front of your house?" I asked.

"Yeah, remember? My mom found it, and that's how we knew who these women were," Bea replied, as I'd thought she would.

"Okay, but correct me if I'm wrong. We identified all the symbols, but I don't remember seeing this one on the one outside your house. The whole pattern is just slightly different here. There is a tail on this, and it's attached to a tiny triangle. Even if we were studying these things, that's a negligible detail."

"It was drawn in chalk," Bea admitted. "I didn't expect it to be as perfect as this one is."

"True," I said. I was about to shrug it off as bad drawing skills on the part of the Sect of Symmetry members. But one word in the text of the description caught my eye. *Dolus.*

"What are you looking at?" Bea asked as I stared at the text.

"Dolus. That means fraud, right? Or hoax?" I asked.

"That's right." Bea immediately looked worried.

"According to the fine, fine print, this image is often used as a decoy for witches looking to gain access to certain properties or areas where the psychic energy is strongest. It looks like a salutation when in reality it is a caveat to keep other witches away." I looked at Bea. "Why would they want other witches to stay away from you? I'm the one they are treating like a redheaded stepchild."

"Cath, I'm scared." Bea instinctively rubbed her belly. "If it were any other time, I'd be ready to fight, but now I'm—"

"You are full of baby. I know, Bea." I took her hand. "And with your mom out of sorts, we are a little short-staffed. But what do we do when we are short-staffed at the café?"

"We're never short-staffed at the café." Bea frowned.

"Okay, you are totally ruining my pep talk. We make do, and we survive. Right? Isn't that what we do when we are short-staffed? You make do with what you have. And right now, what you have is me. As sad as that may sound, I do believe you could do worse." I squared my shoulders and held up my chin.

"Cath, you can't go confront those people alone," Bea said.

"Well, that's true. That's why I'm not going to confront them. I'm going into stealth mode. And I won't be going alone." Just then, Treacle appeared in the doorway. "My secret weapon." I smirked, and Treacle meowed.

"But what are you going to do?" Bea asked.

"First, I need to do a little more research on this Sect of Symmetry. This can't be the only entry in all your mom's library on this group." I got up and started scouring the books. I found three old, dusty tomes that looked as if they hadn't been touched in years. I handed one to Bea, and I started to flip through the others.

"Sorry, Cath. This one is recipes," Bea said, handing back an old, crusty book that I had been sure had to contain some kind of history of every coven in existence since the earth cooled. Then I saw the faded cauldron and the spoon on the cover with the words *Eat, Drink, and Desserts* almost completely worn off.

"Oh, okay. Well, why don't you pick something for dinner," I said.

"Speaking of which. What time is it?" Bea said.

I should have known she'd suddenly be hungry, and when she cracked open the book and began to read, I knew I'd be in for it.

"It's almost five," I replied.

"I'm going to find something to eat. Are you hungry?" she asked as she awkwardly rolled to her side, got to one knee, and pushed herself up.

"No. I'm good."

The truth was that I was not good. I had randomly opened one of the other books and found the exact image of what those Sect of Symmetry nerds had put outside Bea's house. My blood froze in my veins. But I smiled as I looked at Bea and waited for her to leave the room.

"What's wrong?" Treacle came slinking up to me.

"You aren't going to believe this. Not only are these witches the only ones who feel cats are more powerful dead than alive but... they believe in human sacrifice."

I looked to the door, hoping the color would stay in my cheeks so Bea wouldn't notice I was freaking out. These were the kinds of witches that gave the rest of us a bad name. It had been one thing in the olden days to grab the town drunk or a crooked politician and use them as a sacrifice. But the Sect of Symmetry didn't work that way.

"Do you think that's what they want Astrid for?" Treacle asked.

"No." I swallowed, but there was practically no spit in my mouth. *"I think they want her because she's powerful. But they want Bea more."*

"Bea?" Treacle lowered his head.

"Well, not Bea. Bea's baby."

15

SEER

"**A**re they going to try and kill Bea's baby?" Treacle's fur stood on end, and I saw his claws extend and retract as he looked at me.

"*Not quite.*" I let out a deep breath as I kept reading. "*According to this, they need a newborn baby to sort of usher in this doomsday, during which they'll be put in charge of everything. Can you imagine that group of weirdos being in charge of anything? They can't even coordinate their décor, let alone rally the forces of darkness to do their bidding.*"

Treacle wrapped around my leg then looked up at me again, carefully sniffing the corner of the book I was reading. "*What do they do with the baby?*"

"*From what I can tell, the baby becomes the leader, but it won't be Bea's baby on the inside. It'll be possessed by what-*

ever this thing is that they've been paving the way for," I said telepathically. There was no way I was going to discuss this out loud.

"This doesn't sound good," Treacle meowed.

"No. It doesn't." I kept reading and snapped my fingers just as Bea came back into the library with a plate piled high with cheese, grapes, an apple, some crackers, and a huge dill pickle.

"Did you find something?" Bea asked with a mouth full of apple.

"I did," I said as I reached over and snagged one of her crackers. "It says here that this group needs to gather the strength of an interdimensional seer in order to show the way to the blind beast that they are summoning."

The last thing I wanted was for Bea to get ahold of this book and read what I had just told Treacle.

"That's why they need Mom." Bea's eyes bulged as she chewed her food.

"Looks that way." I kept reading and swallowed hard. "It also says that if the seer is part of the coven, that will ensure the coven's place at the head of the table. But if they have to forcefully use the seer, the coven's power will be significantly reduced."

"That's odd. So all they need is for my mom to join the coven, and they get more power?" Bea asked.

"They could have just asked her instead of going through all this rigmarole."

I cleared my throat. "It's not that easy."

"It never is," Bea replied before stuffing some more apple into her face.

"If she willingly joins, she has to go through a thing they call the shredding of the heart." I frowned as I read the description of this horrific ritual, which involved reducing oneself to nothing more than a piece of meat for the witches to feast on.

"What does it say?" Bea asked.

"You don't want to know," I replied, but I kept reading. "If she doesn't willingly join, the coven will acquire her piece by piece, starting with her sleep. They deprive her of sleep, and that allows them to manipulate her more easily. Then her appetite is hijacked, and they feed her food that will slow her body down. Then her thoughts are appropriated by cutting her hair. It is used in a ritual three days after cutting it."

"Cath, this sounds crazy. My mom would never be part of this kind of thing. I can't believe she'd even give them a chance to get inside her head," Bea said, shaking her head at her half-devoured plate of food.

"No. But I saw a documentary once on cults, and this sounds like good old-fashioned brainwashing with a twist of the occult thrown in," I said. "Those poor people who drank the Kool-Aid were sleep deprived, starved, manipulated. It's no different here, except instead of nine hundred and nine people dying, it will just be one. But then again, we don't know how many died before your mom."

"That's a gruesome thought," Bea added. "I almost lost my appetite."

"Almost," I said as I watched her take a big bite out of her pickle.

"Oh my gosh! Cath! Just remember how those witches got the Gingerbread House." Bea clamped her hand over her mouth. "Jake and Blake are dealing with the deaths there right now. And what about the house down the block? You don't think these women are the reason for the sudden outbreak of domestic violence, do you? Oh, Cath. What if the boys are in trouble?"

"We can find out with a simple phone call," I said and tried to roll my eyes at the notion that our men were in anything other than full control of the situation. Nonetheless, I went with Bea into the kitchen, the book I was reading tucked under my arm for safekeeping. She picked up the phone and called the precinct.

"Detective Jake Johnson, please." She nodded and waited for a moment. Within seconds, she let out a sigh of relief, and her eyes rolled in her head. "Hi. No,

I'm fine. I was just checking up on you. Is Blake there with you? He is? Great. Okay, that's all we needed to know."

After a few more words of lovey-dovey-ness, Bea hung up but not before arguing with Jake about who loved who more and how the baby was kicking and how hungry Bea would be when Jake finally got home.

"They are both okay. Under a mountain of paper-work and some loose ends but safe at the station," Bea said.

"What kind of loose ends?" I asked.

They were, after all, looking into these witches, albeit from a different angle than we were and completely unaware of what they were getting into. But it made a lot of sense now that I thought about it. If these women were willing to do what they were doing to Aunt Astrid, what did they care about some strangers killing themselves? Still, what did the houses have to do with them, if anything?

"Jake said the injuries to the victims didn't match up with what they originally thought had happened."

"That's strange," I replied but didn't go into it with her. After what I had read in the book that was under my arm, I wouldn't put anything past this group. And just because the guys were at the station didn't mean they were safe.

❧ 16 ❧

WATERMELON

Bea was fixing herself some calming tea when I had an idea. I held the book close to me, and Treacle came to stand at my feet.

"We're going to go back to that house—Treacle and me. What I want you to do is stay here and keep an eye on your mom. Don't open the door for anyone but us. I'll be back."

I was sure the authority in my voice would be enough to get Bea to fall right in line and just say no problem. Of course, she didn't.

"You can't go back to that house alone. I'll go with you." I saw Bea swallow hard.

"What? In your condition?" I pointed to her big belly. "Sure. It'll be no different from running a race carrying a full-sized watermelon under your shirt. No one will see or hear you."

"But you can't go alone," she pleaded.

"Why? I've done lots of things alone. Bea, I live alone. I am fully capable of handling those witches alone. In fact, I've dealt with scarier things than them alone. Remember Darla from high school? She was scarier than them. How about Tom Warner's mom? She was scarier than them. That spider in the café? Much, much scarier than them." That one made me shiver.

"No. It's not a good idea," Bea insisted.

"Yeah, and you coming with is?" I snapped before softening my glare at my overly emotional pregnant cousin. "Bea, someone has to stay with your mom. Plus, you've got that baby to think about."

Just then, we heard footsteps on the porch, a knock on the door, and the jingle of keys. The door opened, only to be held fast by that tiny, flimsy chain.

"Hey. What's going on in there?" It was Jake.

"Oh my gosh!" I shouted as I stomped to the door to open it. "You gave me a heart attack!" I put my hand over my chest and slipped the book onto another bookcase by the door, hoping Bea wouldn't pay any attention to it as Jake and Blake came in.

"I gave you a heart attack? We went home and found the door unlocked, no one home, and no food in the fridge. How's my two favorite babies?" Jake said as he sauntered up to Bea, who smiled with tears brimming in her eyes as she wrapped her arms around Jake for a long hug. She was *so* pregnant.

"What's the matter?" Blake asked me quietly.

"We've got a problem," I whispered and looked deeply into his eyes. "Jake, can you stay with Bea and Aunt Astrid for a while?"

"Yeah. We were coming home to get something to eat before going over to the Gingerbread House to do a little snooping around. There are some things about those domestic violence incidents and suicides that aren't matching up," Blake said in his usual monotone.

"That's funny you should say that. That is where I was going too."

I told him about the book and Aunt Astrid and my hunch that there was a lot more going on than just a group of women living together and selling their pitiful wares at the art fair.

"So, what is your plan?" Blake asked.

"Hold on tight," I replied. "Jake, would you mind staying here with Bea and Aunt Astrid while Blake and I go run an errand?"

"Cath, don't even think about it," Bea said.

"Think about what? Blake needs some... um, plastic baggies, and we're going to the store to get some. We'll be back later."

I didn't wait for her to reply before I grabbed

Blake's arm and pulled him out the door. Just before it closed, Treacle slipped out and came to my side, meowing.

"Are you sure this is a good idea?" Blake asked.

"No," I replied matter-of-factly and looked at him as if he had just asked if I wanted pineapple and ham on my pizza. "But it's all we've got, and if my hunch is right, we don't have a lot of time."

"I love how you look when you start to get witchy. Your cheeks glow and your eyes twinkle," Blake said in his straitlaced, stoic sort of way without a trace of a smile on his face. "I'm sure it's just the increase in blood being pumped when you decide you're going to do something dangerous, maybe even life-threatening, but I can't help but think danger looks good on you."

"Maybe I should join the police force," I replied.

"I don't know if you meet the height requirement," Blake replied without emotion.

"I'm not that short," I muttered before pointing to Treacle, who was heading off ahead of us. *"Where do you think you're going?"*

"I'll meet you at the house. Good luck," Treacle said before he slunk out of sight into some bushes.

"Stay out of sight. You know what they think about cats!" I replied before getting into Blake's car. I was hopeful none of the witches would recognize his car.

Within fifteen minutes, we were positioned down the street from the Gingerbread House. Crouched in the seats like a couple of Peeping Toms, Blake and I spied on it.

"Hey, that For Sale sign in front of that house," I whispered as I pointed across the street. "That wasn't there yesterday."

"So?" Blake asked as he reached across me to the glove box and pulled a pair of binoculars out. "People put their homes up for sale all the time."

"Yeah, but I was just here yesterday, and it wasn't. And how many houses have gone up for sale on this street since these women moved into my Gingerbread House?" I whispered. "And you said something was fishy with the deaths that had occurred here too. It's like the houses were already bought before they were even listed for sale. Don't tell me that doesn't sound odd."

"You are correct." Blake cleared his throat as he looked through the binoculars. "And that doesn't include the death we were informed of this morning. Jake and I were on our way out here to talk to the neighbors. He wanted to check on Bea."

"Another death? What house?" I asked, looking down the simple, stereotypical suburban street.

Then I was hit with an idea. I grabbed a crumpled receipt from the side console and pulled a pen from

Blake's breast pocket. I drew a rough map of the street, labelling the houses where there was either a death or a For Sale sign.

"We've got the Gingerbread House. The one across the street. The new For Sale sign you just pointed out. And now the elderly man at the house two doors down from that." He pointed to a quaint ranch-style home.

"Elderly man?" I said, feeling bad. It was one thing to pick on people who might be able to defend themselves, but these witches had a thing for seasoned citizens like my aunt and this man Blake was talking about. It was as bad as their dislike for cats. Something was wrong with a person if they didn't have a soft spot in their heart for animals and old people.

"He was a bachelor by the name of Bob Zarowny. Like a lot of older people, he contacted the police every once in a while when he heard a strange sound or thought he saw something suspicious," Blake said. "But we got a call from the neighbors that his garage door had been left open for two days."

"Oh no," I said, feeling my throat tighten.

"It just didn't seem right," Blake said. "When we got there, the man had already been dead for over twenty-four hours. At first, it was thought his heart just wound down, even with the expression on his face."

"Expression?" I asked.

"Yeah. He looked like he was scared. Terrified, actually," Blake said before launching into some scientific reason the muscles in the body move independently during a stroke or heart attack and can cause the deceased to look like they've seen a walking nightmare before finally succumbing to the Grim Reaper. But I didn't buy it. Not in this case.

"What made you think there was something more sinister going on?" I asked.

"Well, the fact that the neighbors had heard him shouting the night before. They said it sounded like he was having a fight with someone. But he lived alone. There was no car in the driveway. Nothing," Blake said and put down his binoculars.

I didn't know what to say. Maybe the old man had just died of a heart attack. Maybe he'd had a bout of dementia at the end, although I'd never heard of such a thing happening. No one ever just had a touch of dementia all of a sudden out of the blue. For some reason, hearing about this old man being all alone to possibly deal with those witches made me feel bad, like something had sunk deep in my chest.

I looked down at the paper and pen in my hand to see if there was any kind of pattern. My Aunt

Astrid and Bea both lived across the street from me, making a simple triangle if anyone was to have a bird's-eye view. When I included the new house for sale and the old man's house that didn't have a sign in the yard yet, at first I didn't see anything. But then I drew a line from the Gingerbread House, the first one occupied by this group, and drew a line to the next house where a death had occurred.

"Oh my," I said.

"What is it?" Blake asked.

"Well, If I'm looking at this right, it looks like a crude image of an old Masonic symbol." I swallowed hard. "You know how some kids in high school think they are cool when they scribble pentagrams in their notebooks? Everyone knows what a pentagram stands for, or thinks they do. It's evil, dangerous. Okay, if they really knew anything, they'd know that a pentagram was no scarier than a smiley face compared to this Masonic symbol called a Kly."

"I've never heard of such a thing," Blake said.

"No. Of course you haven't. They don't teach this in schools. I learned about it from my aunt." My chest tightened as I thought about what was happening to her and hoped she wasn't giving Bea and Jake a hard time. "Just like normal parents frown on their kids having anything that looks like a pentagram in their possession, that is what witches think of the Kly."

I was just about to go into detail about why this symbol was right up there with swastikas and the number 666 when we both froze. The witches were on the move.

❧ 17 ❧

DIABOLICAL REASONS

A s the sun inched closer to the horizon, setting off a beautiful sunset, Blake and I inched down in our seats so as not to be noticed. We watched as Cedar led the witches out of the Gingerbread House. She stood at the edge of the driveway as the others scattered in all directions, reminding me of the anthill Treacle had said he watched. They didn't bother looking around. Peabody Street was rife with the activity pouring out from that house. This was the perfect time to go see what was happening in the shed.

"Okay, I'm going around back. There's something I need to check," I said as I rolled down the car window with one hand while reaching back into the glovebox for the tiny LED flashlight I knew was in there. It fit snugly into my pocket.

"What are you talking about?" Blake took hold of my wrist. "You're not going anywhere."

"They are all out of the house. There is something in the backyard I need to check out. I'll be perfectly safe," I said. "I'm going to crawl out the window so I don't have to open the car door. Your doors squeak."

"Cath, you aren't doing any such thing," Blake insisted.

"Blake, I know we are dating, and I couldn't be happier, but that doesn't mean you get to step in and tell me what I can or can't do," I whispered. "I want to make you happy, and I want you to know that I value everything you say. But if my family needs my help, neither you nor anyone else can stop me from doing what I can to help them."

"You want to make me happy?" Blake smirked.

"Of course I do." I rolled my eyes. "But this isn't the time or place. I have to check out the backyard."

"Cath, you can't."

"Now, what did I just say about telling me what to do? Didn't you listen? I—"

Blake put his index finger to his lips then pointed to the Gingerbread House. Up in the top window was a dark form peeking outside. Instantly, I remembered the fingers stretching out underneath the door when I had gone snooping around. The house wasn't empty, and there was an all-seeing thing up on the second floor.

"I've got to get to the shed, Blake. And I don't have all night to wait," I said, looking at the creepy round window with the thing in it.

"Yeah, and I have to interview the neighbors about the death of the old man," Blake said. "As far as these women know, I'm just a cop doing my job."

"Oh, Blake, if you go snooping around now while they're all out there, they might gang up on you. Going into the backyard will be safer than that," I said, my eyebrows furrowed at him.

Blake was smart, but I wasn't sure if he really grasped the power these women had been stockpiling. If they'd done what they had to Aunt Astrid, Blake was no match for them. He was walking into a gunfight with a knife.

"I'm not going to do anything but run interference." He looked in the rearview mirror and then at me. "When I get out of the car and approach the house next door—where, as far as we know, normal people still live—you sneak out of the car. But don't run across the street from here. Go down a few houses and double back. Make it look like you escaped from the car, not like you were going to peep in someone's windows."

I smiled and couldn't stop myself from giving

Blake a deep, wonderful kiss. It gave me that extra rush of adrenaline I was going to need to sneak into Cedar's backyard. She was still standing at the edge of the driveway, her creepy ice-blue eyes watching her minions.

With the grace and stealth of a hippo in a pool of mud, I slipped out of the car window as Blake got out on his side, coughing and slamming the door shut without worry about who would see him. His goal was to get all eyes on him as I made a break for it. Thankfully, he made a ruckus that hid the facts that I nearly broke my ankle as I landed funny, let out a cuss as I crouched behind the car, and bumped my chin on the open window. I was so aggravated with myself that I almost stood straight up and yelled to Cedar that I was marching into her backyard and she could go ahead and try and stop me. But I didn't when I realized Blake's plan had worked, and all eyes were on him. Even whatever was casting a shadow on the second floor was gazing in his direction.

Just as I ran across the street, I saw a familiar shadow slinking behind some bushes.

"There is a back entrance to the fence. Follow me," Treacle said.

He led me through the neighbor's yard and all the way around the privacy fence that enclosed the Gingerbread House's backyard. Sure enough, there was a second set of hinges. What was even better was that this was just feet from the shed, where I needed to be anyway.

"Good job," I whispered to Treacle. "Now you should skedaddle. This is a dangerous place for cats."

"I'm not leaving you. There is a foul smell in the air. Like the smell around Astrid," Treacle replied stubbornly.

"Fine," I replied. *"It's not like I can tell you what to do. So let's get this done quick."*

I jiggled the gate and heard the latch on the other side. Treacle looked up at me, and before I could even think a thought, he jumped up and peered over the top.

"Ugh. They've got it padlocked," Treacle reported.

"I should have known it wouldn't be easy," I mumbled. "Is anyone around?"

Treacle's green eyes narrowed. *"Not a soul."*

I didn't have a lot of time, and sneaking in this way was a lot more practical than actually trying to sneak in the front gate that faced the street, which had been my original idea. So, after a few quick breaths, I reached up, took hold of the pointed wood at the top of the fence, braced one foot against the planks, and, with all the strength in my skinny arms, pulled myself up.

It was a horrible scene that I hoped no one was watching. My face was drenched in sweat and bright red as I grunted my way up to the pointy top, trying to place my stomach between the slats so as not to stab myself. It wasn't working well. Before I could pull my leg over to straddle the fence, gravity stepped in and yanked me to the ground. I was sure I'd woken the dead as my breath was knocked out of me and I gasped for air.

"Anyone hear me?" I looked up at Treacle, who was surveying the estate.

"I don't think so."

I nodded, pushed myself up to my knees, and slowly stood, taking inventory of my limbs to make sure nothing was sprained or broken. The only thing damaged was my ego. So I quickly stepped behind the shed and collected myself. After a couple deep breaths more, I peeked around and saw that the yard was completely empty and the blinds to the patio doors were pulled tightly shut. The windows that faced the backyard were also covered by curtains. Thankfully, there was no rear-facing bedroom window to allow the thing in the upstairs room to peer down at me. Confidently, I reached for the shed door only to find it had a padlock on it too.

"What the...? Grr," I muttered and clenched my teeth.

Quickly, I disappeared around the back of the

shed to try and come up with another plan. I looked at Treacle, who was still perched on the fence.

"*What is it?*" he asked.

"Another padlock," I whispered.

"*Try the window,*" Treacle replied, motioning with his head.

As I turned around, there it was: a plexiglass window that was simply snapped into place. My eyes lit up. I tried to peer inside but could barely make out anything. There was no alternative but to break the window. I put both hands on the glass and pushed as hard as I could. One corner buckled and bent inward. Then another gave way. With two corners free, I was able to bend the window until the frame snapped, and the whole thing cracked apart. I turned and gave a thumbs-up to Treacle.

It was snug, but I was able to get into the shed a lot more easily than I had gotten over the fence. But once I was in, I regretted it.

The smell was awful. A sweet, pungent aroma hit me. Add to that stifling heat and a weird sound like someone loudly smacking their lips, and my stomach folded over on itself. I pulled out the flashlight and snapped it on while I pulled the collar of my shirt over my nose.

In front of me was a sheet suspended from the low ceiling. On the other side was a faint glow that looked like candlelight. It was enough to highlight the stained and dirty cloth that partially separated the tiny space into two sections. Carefully, I stepped around it and shined the flashlight on the other side. I gasped. The beam of the light began to shake as I trembled.

Spread on a small wooden table were strange bowls of rotting fruit and raw meat. Flies buzzed all over the place, and the weird smacking sound turned out to be bugs burrowing in the rotting stuff. Now, I know there are lots of traditions that include such offerings as part of their rituals. But none that I would ever encourage anyone to join includes the symbol of the woman in the triangle holding a cat by the throat like this one did. It sent a shiver up my spine as I looked at it, making me feel like something had been taken away from me. I couldn't *un*see it.

There was something else strewn all over the altar. At first, my heart raced when I thought it was spider webs, but on closer inspection, I came to the sad realization that it was my aunt's hair. The beautiful silver and gray locks that Cedar had convinced her to cut off were strewn all over this sick, disgusting smorgasbord. Part of me wanted to collect it all and burn it or bring it home—anything other than leave it here on this table of nightmares. But just as I was about to try and collect it without touching any of the foul stuff, I heard voices approaching.

My heart began to race again. I snapped off my flashlight and stuck it in my pocket. Quickly and carefully, I slipped back behind the curtain and ducked beneath the table. Before I realized this was a bad idea, my foot stepped into something gooey and gushy that had dripped down from the table. My whole body recoiled as the gross texture reverberated against my shoe, through my foot, and up my leg. I swallowed hard, pulled my shirt higher up over my nose, and held my breath. The sound of keys in the lock scared me as I looked out the small window I had broken. I was sure that if they were to see it, they would search this entire shed. This was hardly a refuge.

Before I could make the jump out the window, the door opened wide. The wave of fresh air made me feel as if I'd taken a shower. It invigorated me, and I was able to concentrate, see more clearly, and make a plan, which was to sit tight for the time being. But when I heard the witches start talking, I grew ready for war.

"Remember, this is for Astrid to usher in the Kly." I recognized Cedar's voice.

"We've got to get to her. None of this will be

worth it if she isn't brought into the fold." I was sure that was Ethel's voice.

"It won't be long. She's been tainted. There won't be anything those two girls can do to help her. And the baby is a boy," Cedar hissed. "It's a sign we've chosen wisely."

I couldn't help it; my heart leapt a tiny bit at that news. I had known Bea was having a boy. I'd just had a gut feeling she was. And I also knew that it was going to take more than some Armageddon-welcoming coven to get me to sit this one out.

Just knowing that baby was part of their cere-mony made my blood boil. Sure, Aunt Astrid was powerful, and they wanted her for diabolical reasons. And Bea was the most compassionate and wonderful empath a person could know. But to go after that baby, who hadn't even had a chance to become himself yet—well, that was just low. And I wasn't going to let fear get in my way of stopping them.

WOLF SPIDER

"Now, get in position," Cedar ordered. "We must beg the Kly to bring our sisters here by safe passage. We have but one more house to acquire, and then the ball will be in motion."

"All hail the Kly," Luann said in her bubbly, schoolteacherish voice. They all began to chant, "All hail the Kly."

And then, as if holding some twisted church service, they began to chant about this creature they would soon be pulling into our dimension. It was all-seeing and all-knowing. Its right hand was insanity and its left was chaos, and with its guidance, these women would rule the world.

It could have been the fact that I was sitting on a cold slab of concrete, or maybe it was the creepy things I was hearing from these broads that made me shiver. But I was sure the temperature in the little shack was getting colder and the stench was getting stronger, and I wasn't sure how much longer I was going to be able to keep my composure.

"Bring Astrid Greenstone to our fold. Smite anyone who gets in her way. Even if it must be done by her own hand. She will be your guide. Your humble attendant. In your service for eternity. In return for her, you will give us your favor and protection," Cedar chanted.

Again, they all started chanting and stomping their feet, and it kept getting colder and colder. But I didn't dare move a muscle. I didn't want to take any chance that these women might have superhuman hearing or anything.

"Soon, Shelia will be ready, and you will take your bride," Cedar hissed.

Those words lodged in my ears. Just when I thought I couldn't get any colder, my blood turned to ice. Who was Shelia? What kind of arranged marriage was this? Could it be someone who would be moving into that last house they needed to acquire? Was it someone's cousin? I didn't want to admit that it was probably that thing with the long gray fingers that had tried to reach me. Just the memory of that made me tremble more than the cold.

Then, as if my predicament couldn't get any worse, I looked down and, in the pale light of the candles, saw, just inches from my hand, my old nemesis: the wolf spider. It was bigger than the one at the café that had nearly killed me. This one was black and stood out against the gray concrete. It appeared to be confronting me, as if it was ready to settle a score, raising one front appendage into the air as if it was challenging me, daring me to do something. Then a second front appendage went up. This thing was not just an ordinary wolf spider. As much as I hated to admit it, I had heard that arachnids are more frightened of us than we are of them. This one, however, obviously had not heard that same information.

Then, like a bolt, I remembered Cedar being in the café that day I was nearly killed by the spider in the storage area. She had had one in her hair that had disappeared as quickly as I'd seen it. Was this the same one?

It inched closer to the hand that was flat against the concrete slab, supporting my weight. I was cramped beneath the table as it was, and any sudden move could give me away. Cold sweat began to form down the middle of my back as the spider inched closer and closer until I could feel the weight of one of its legs touching my finger. It wasn't heavy or painful, but that didn't matter. I was sure that any second this thing would dart up my arm and get underneath my shirt, its eight legs all maneuvering at lightning speed to carry its bulbous body toward my jugular vein. This wasn't just a spider trying to get from one dark, dank corner to another. This beast was on a mission to expose me to its master.

A scream rose up from the bottom of my belly, and I was afraid I was going to lose control—stand up, knock over the altar, and run around in circles as this primitive coven of witches watched before turning me into some kind of stuttering dunce for their amusement. All because of a spider.

I bit the inside of my cheek, hoping the pain would bring me away from the edge of this crazy phobia. I thought of Aunt Astrid and what these women had done to her. My breath came back, and I hadn't even known I had been holding it at the time. Then I thought of Bea and the baby boy, my nephew, that she was carrying.

And in one swift movement, I squashed the spider and pushed aside my revulsion at the way its body popped beneath my hand. I did it fast. The arachnid felt nothing. I felt everything. But it was gone now.

And as soon as I did that, the chanting stopped.

"Someone's here," Ethel said.

"Yes. Very close by," Cedar muttered.

"Shelia is in the kitchen," Hannah said.

"What is she doing down there?" Cedar growled.

"Her *loftiness* said she was hungry. Again," Hannah replied. "She's getting out of hand."

"Go get her back upstairs. Make sure she has whatever she wants," Cedar said. It sounded as if her teeth were clenched.

"Fine," Hannah huffed before storming out of the shed.

"Where are they?" Cedar asked.

"I don't know. But close. Very close," Ethel said.

I expected them to yank up the tablecloth and peer at me all at once. But it didn't happen. Instead, they dashed out of the shed, leaving me there with squashed spider on my hand and the urge to run sweeping through my body.

After swallowing hard, I finally crawled out from under the altar. I could still hear their voices, but I was sure they were far enough away from the shed for me to at least slip behind it and pull myself over the fence unnoticed. I had gotten over once, right? Plus, I had darkness in my favor now that the sun had gone down. The yard would be darker, and no one would notice me just slip out the shed door. Without thinking, I wiped the remains of the spider on my pants, feeling as if I could face anything now that I had confronted my fear of the eight-legged devils and won. Carefully, I stepped out of the shed.

But all good plans are usually thwarted, and this one was no exception. They were all there. Staring at me.

All the witches from the barbeque stood facing me in cheap black robes. They were gathered around a pit of smoldering embers that were just beginning to glow.

It probably wasn't a smart move. In fact, the more I thought I'd be poking the bear, the closer the stick inched to the beast's hind end. Finally, I couldn't resist anymore.

"Bwahahaha!" I laughed. No, I didn't just laugh. I pointed and laughed. "You've got to be kidding me! *The Witches of Eastwick* movie was more believable than you are in those robes!"

Apparently, they didn't see the humor in what I was saying. To be honest, I suddenly became acutely aware that not only were they not laughing, but they weren't even fazed. The weight of their stare started to freak me out. I chuckled, put my hands on my hips, shifted from my left leg to my right, licked my dry lips, and cleared my throat.

"Go ahead and mock us. You aren't even a real witch," Cedar hissed.

"You have no power," Hannah growled, her crooked eye staring off in a completely different direction.

"You think because you have the Greenstone name you have somehow acquired their mysticism. You are a phony. The powers skipped over you, holding you in contempt as a failure, an afterthought that can be brushed away like dust from an old book," Luann said in her high-pitched, Minnie Mouse voice. "There is no use for you. You are nothing."

I could remember being told the same things by Darla in high school. She had hated me for no good reason and had made it a point to remind me of that fact every day. Even now, when I saw her in town or when she came bustling into the cafe, with her perfectly manicured nails and her ex-husband's alimony keeping her in a comfortable lifestyle, I could remember those words. But they no longer bothered me like they used to. And I certainly wasn't going to let some Halloween costume–wearing *Mean Girls* club get to me.

"Treacle? Are you still here?" I called.

"Where else would I be?"

"*Any of your friends around?*" I asked, my heart racing as I waited for his answer.

"*Always.*" Treacle's meow was like a lion's roar to me. I smirked as I watched the look on the witches' faces.

Just then, a huge crow landed on the post.

"*Are you here to help?*" I asked the sleek bird.

"*Why not,*" he replied and then cawed loudly.

Within seconds, another crow landed, and another and another, until the entire top of the fence was nearly covered in black-feathered birds, squawking and flapping their wings. Overhead, a few hoot owls swooped dangerously close to the women, who ducked and hissed at them.

Treacle, appearing from the shadows, slunk up to me, rubbing his head affectionately against my leg. He had led a small army of alley cats to hop up on the fence, next to their feathered brethren, in a sign of solidarity against the witches.

"What's happening?" Luann choked.

"Where are they coming from?" Ethel tugged at Cedar's robe. Cedar yanked her arm away while her icy blue eyes stayed glued to mine.

"Your move," I said coldly.

"So, you have a few birds and cats at your disposal," Cedar said, taking a small step toward me. Treacle began to growl. She stopped, looked right at the cat, and swiped at him as if she were a feline too. But it would take a lot more than that to scare my Treacle. Every hair on his body stood up, and he looked like he'd grown five feet. He stared at her as if she was nothing more than a rat trying to intimidate him. His green eyes practically glowed.

"Is everyone ready?" I called out telepathically.

Every nerve in my body was on edge. Like a rubber band stretched to the breaking point, I listened as all my furry and feathered friends waited for the call. In a chorus of caws, meows, hisses, and growls, I got my answer.

"Now!" I shouted.

Every animal dove into the yard as if there was a free-for-all on birdseed and raw tuna. To my pleasant surprise, several plump raccoons also poured themselves over the fence while mice as small as half dollars scurried under it. They swooped and scuttled all over the yard.

The witches screamed and swung their arms and kicked their feet, sending some of the animals flying. They swatted at the crows, successfully knocking a few to the ground, but where one went down, there were two more to defend it.

"Let's go!" I shouted over the noise to Treacle, who darted toward the other gate across the yard.

I was just a few steps behind when my foot caught

on a branch. At least, that was what I thought it was. But when the gray fingers wrapped around my ankle and I could feel the hard bones beneath the papery skin, I knew it wasn't a branch. Terror struck me, and I looked right into the face of Sheila! All I could think was that if she was the blushing bride, I would hate to see what the groom looked like.

"Treacle!" I shouted.

My cat turned around and hissed. Sheila looked up at him and did the same. But her grip on my ankle loosened enough that I was able to yank away and run to the gate. Her arm slowly started to stretch toward us. Treacle hissed, and with every claw extended, he swatted at the witch, making her scream and gurgle.

With the gate open, I ran out. A swarm of crows descended on Sheila, distracting her for long enough that Treacle was able to follow me. We slammed the gate shut, and within seconds, all the animals had taken leave of the horrible place.

My ankle ached as I ran toward Blake's car. He was casually strolling toward it as I started shouting.

"Hurry! Get in the car! Get in the car!" Treacle jumped in the open window. I got in and honked the horn to get Blake to hurry.

"What did you find? Let me guess: they saw you. Is that what all that noise was about?" he asked as he quickly turned the ignition and threw the car into gear.

"They saw us, all right. Didn't they, Treacle?" I reached back and scratched the cat's head. He purred and whipped his tail with excitement.

But just as we were about to peel out of there, ready to burn rubber all the way to Aunt Astrid's house, the engine quit.

❧ 19 ❧

PEABODY STREET

"What's the matter?" I asked as Blake tried the key and pumped the gas pedal.

"I don't know. This has never happened before," he said calmly.

I whirled around and looked out the back window. Like a scene out of a bad 1970s movie, the witches approached the car. For as cheap as their robes looked, they did blend in with the darkness almost seamlessly. Anyone who might casually look out their window wouldn't immediately see them. Plus, half the people on this block had died of a mysterious cause or a suspicious suicide.

"They're getting closer," I muttered. "Blake?"

"Just stay calm," he assured me, but my gut was tightening into a ball, and my heart was racing. My hands started to sweat, and I was sure that I could smell an electricity in the air that hadn't been there before.

"They're getting closer to the car," I said, my voice cracking.

"Okay," Blake replied as he continued to try the ignition.

"What are we going to do?" I was really having a hard time controlling the fear in my voice. I trusted Blake, but this was getting too close. When he looked at me and smirked, I knew he had an idea. It just wasn't a great one.

"Feel like running?" he asked.

"Oh my gosh! Treacle!"

As soon as I opened the car door, my cat was out and took off like a bullet, disappearing underneath some bushes. I was not far behind, but Blake took hold of my hand and nearly dragged me into the wooded area that Treacle had led me through before when we'd escaped the witches' barbecue.

We made it a couple hundred yards into the dark foliage before the terrain made it too dangerous to run. Blake yanked me behind a wide oak tree, wrapped his arms tightly around me, and leaned toward my ear. "Don't move."

I nodded, held my breath, and remained perfectly still.

"Where are they?" Ethel grumbled.

"They couldn't have just disappeared," Luann whined.

"I don't see them at all," Hannah snapped. "You were wrong, Cedar. You said the girl had no powers."

"I wasn't wrong," Cedar hissed. "She has telepathy. Nothing more than that."

"She has telepathy with animals. With cats. You didn't warn us about that. Now what are we going to do?" Hannah continued to poke at Cedar until I heard a loud smack.

"And you'll get worse than that if you continue your insubordination," Cedar snapped. "We'll talk with Sheila. She'll know what to do."

"She's gone!" shouted Louise, who was obviously bringing up the rear.

"Who's gone?" Cedar asked.

"Sheila!" Louise sounded like she was about to cry.

All the witches began to mutter and gasp and whine about what to do next.

"Every one of you shut up!" Cedar replied.

"The time for her wedding is getting closer, and she knows it. I'll bet I know where she's headed. She can feel the pull of her mate, who is circling the doorway Astrid is to break open," Cedar said.

I squeezed Blake's arm, and he did the same to me.

"But if she's out when the sun comes up, everything will be ruined. She has to be back tonight," Luann whined.

"Sheila may be young, but she isn't stupid. If she doesn't come back on her own, which I'm sure she will, we'll find her long before dawn," Cedar said. "We must prepare the other houses and focus on the last one. Hurry. And not another word out of you, Hannah, or the Kly will learn of your disobedience and punish you accordingly."

Blake and I didn't hear anything else, yet we remained still for some time. I couldn't believe what those witches had been saying. I didn't understand all of it, but what I did understand made me desperate to get to Aunt Astrid and Bea.

"Don't worry. We'll get to your family before they do," Blake said as if reading my mind.

We waited for the witches to leave. They scurried back to the Gingerbread House, and before I realized it, Blake and I were back in his car. This time, it started right up.

"Did they put the whammy on your car? Please tell me that sometimes it just doesn't start," I muttered as I tried to distract myself from worrying about Aunt Astrid and Bea.

"It is an old car. But I've never had a problem with it before. It's really rather simple to keep a car running. If you keep the tires inflated, have the oil changed once in a while, and don't speed, it isn't impossible to keep a car running for twenty years. I had a car that I applied those rules to, and—"

"I know you're trying to keep me calm. But it isn't working," I said.

"Don't worry, Cath. They won't get to your family. I promise," Blake replied before rubbing my knee. "Let me tell you what I learned from the neighbors."

I'd forgotten that Blake had actually gone to Peabody Street to investigate the latest in a string of strange deaths. He hadn't gotten much information on the actual deaths, but he certainly had gotten an earful.

Mrs. Liane Stortz and her husband, Ken, had lived on Peabody for over ten years. When Blake had knocked on their door, they were happy to talk. Or maybe a better word was scold. Blake recounted their conversation for me.

"It's about time you guys came by," Ken said, letting Blake into his home after he inspected Blake's badge and identification. It was a simple place with family pictures on the walls and decorative pillows on the couch and love seat.

"Who is it, Ken?"

"It's the police, Liane!" Ken shouted to the voice that came from somewhere else in the house.

"It's about time!" she shouted back, and Blake heard footsteps pounding up a flight of stairs. Within a few seconds, a woman at least a foot shorter than Mr. Stortz appeared with her hand on her hip.

"This is my wife," Ken said.

"Are you guys going to do something about what's going on?" Liane snapped.

"That's what I'm here to ask about. What can you tell me about the death of your neighbor?" Blake asked.

"Our neighbor? Which one?" Ken chuckled. "They're all dead. And if they aren't dead, they're moving. Did you see the For Sale signs in all the yards? It's like there is an epidemic, and we're just waiting to see if we come down with a case of suicide too."

"Yeah, we don't have the luxury to just pick up and move," Liane said, folding her arms over her chest.

"No, ma'am," Blake said.

Listening to the story, I felt bad for him and the Stortzes. None of them really knew what they were up against. Fear could turn to anger as easily as boiling water into steam.

They didn't invite Blake to sit down, but they did

begin by telling him something I was sure he already knew: all the trouble had started when the family in the Gingerbread House had died. That was ground zero for the rash of deaths on their block.

"We've seen the people that moved in there. At first, we thought they were just an eccentric family. But they skulk around, and when they had their barbecue, there were weird goings-on there," Ken said.

"Real weird." Liane nodded.

"Can you tell me what you saw?" Blake asked.

"Look, we've heard yelling, singing, chanting..." Ken said.

"Yeah, chanting," Liane confirmed. "At all hours of the night. We could be dead asleep and suddenly there would be a scream. We've called the police."

"And what did the police do?" Blake asked.

"They'd take our information and go to the house we heard the scream from. It's been a different house the last couple times we heard it," Ken replied.

"Did it come from your older neighbor's house?" Blake pointed to the house to the left of the Stortzes', where the last victim had lived.

"Yeah, but by that time, we'd stopped calling. The police would come talk to us then go to the house we heard noises from. If someone answered the door, the police would talk to them and then come back with some fairy story that they were watching a scary movie or saw a mouse." Ken rolled his eyes.

"I've had mice in my house and never screamed like that," Liane added.

"Yeah, we get mice in the fall almost every year. She's terrified of them," Ken said, jerking his thumb in his wife's direction.

"Yeah. I hate them," Liane continued. "But I never screamed like that."

"No. She never screamed like that," Ken added. "Each time the police left, the next day there was another person who was dead. People are leaving the block. We don't have that luxury. We've got family in town. All our friends are here. And moving costs money. We can't just pack up and move like these other people. So, tell me, Detective, are we just waiting for the suicide bug to get to us?"

"What are you guys doing to find out what's happening?" Liane asked.

Blake was taking meticulous notes and then stopped and looked at the couple.

"THEY WERE JUST ORDINARY PEOPLE TRYING TO live their lives with strange and scary deaths all around them. And I had no real answers except that the Wonder Falls P.D. was doing its best to get to the bottom of things." Blake's face twisted in worry as he drove toward my aunt's house. "They took no comfort from my words. I couldn't blame them."

"What did they say next?" I asked.

"Not very much except that they hoped the police would help out before the entire street was wiped out," Blake replied with a sigh as we drove past the café.

"Did any of them speak to the new residents?" I asked. "That coven has moved into the houses faster than termites to a wood pile."

"The Stortzes said they steered clear of all of them," Blake replied. "Once the Gingerbread House was occupied and strange things started happening on the street, Ken and Liane said they saw how all the new residents were hanging out together. It spooked them."

"That would scare me too," I said.

"But aside from not seeing anyone go into or come from their neighbor's house before the occupant died, I came away with nothing," Blake said. "That makes everything even more disturbing. Several people died by suicide who had no history of mental issues and murder-suicides who had no history of domestic violence."

"Those witches are using the residences in order

to get the houses that they need to form their cosmic symbol to usher in this *thing* they worship. I'm afraid if you are looking for regular clues, Blake, you might not find any. If they are anything like the other witches I know, they wouldn't necessarily leave a trace of anything behind. At least, nothing you could see. My Aunt Astrid would be able to see it, but they took her vision from her."

When I said that, Blake snapped his head in my direction. "What did you say?"

"They took my aunt's ability to see other dimensions. They blocked it or suppressed it or something, and now she sees normally, like you and I do. Just this dimension." I swallowed hard. "It has her all off kilter."

Blake clenched his teeth. Aunt Astrid had always treated Blake like family, as if she knew all along that he and I would end up together. It was obvious from his reaction that this case had suddenly become that much more personal, because the perpetrators had harmed my aunt. My heart pounded with such pride that I almost leaned over to kiss him right then.

But when we pulled into the driveway of my aunt's house, my heart pounded for another reason. The door was standing wide open.

BASIC BRAINWASHING

"Oh no!" Before the car even came to a stop, I jumped out and ran inside. "Aunt Astrid! Bea!" I shouted.

Before I could dash up the stairs, Marshmallow appeared from behind a curtain. From underneath the couch, Peanut Butter made his appearance. And as if the whole thing had been choreographed, Treacle slunk in behind me, having taken a different route through the neighborhood than Blake and I had.

"Are they here?" Blake asked as he came up immediately behind me.

"What happened?" I asked, feeling sick to my stomach.

"Jake took Astrid and Bea to the police station," Marsh-

mallow said. *"Something about evidence back from the lab and he had to get there."*

"Do you know anything about evidence you and Jake were waiting on?" I looked at Blake. His eyes widened.

"The evidence is back from the lab?"

I nodded.

"Come on. We might not have a Ouija board or tarot cards to help us. It might just boil down to good old-fashioned forensics."

Blake grabbed my hand, and we streamed out of my aunt's house like a train. Blake, Marshmallow, Peanut Butter, Treacle, and I all jumped into his car and headed for the police station.

But getting there wasn't going to be as easy as driving through town late in the evening with almost no traffic. There was something following us, something I had seen before—and it had seen me.

"Sheila," I muttered.

"What?" Blake asked.

"Remember when we were hiding in the woods? The witches said Sheila was gone. Well, there she is," I said and pointed at the upcoming streetlight. Underneath it was the cloaked figure, the hood pulled back just enough to reveal the shriveled face behind it. I could see a row of teeth as she stood there, smiling at us as we passed. I'd expected her teeth to be crooked and decayed like her face seemed to be. But they weren't. They were big and shiny, and there were too many in her mouth.

"What is that?" Blake gasped as we sped past.

"You'll get another glimpse of her up there." I pointed to the next spotlight. Sheila was under that lamppost too. This time she was closer to the street and was laughing at us as we zoomed past.

"Is she trying to beat us somewhere?" Blake asked.

"I don't know. The witches said to let her have her fun. I'm not sure what that entails. Perhaps forcing a car to swerve into oncoming traffic is what she has in mind." I swallowed hard. "Maybe we should get out and run?"

Just then, I saw the figure once again step out of the shadows at the next lamppost and step into the street. Blake slowed to swerve away from her, and she desperately reached, scratched, and clawed at Jake's car, laughing at us the entire time.

"I see you, Cath!" she howled. "I can't wait to eat your cats!"

"W-what did she just say?" I stuttered.

"She's trying to scare you, Cath," Blake said.

I looked into the back seat at all my beloved familiars and clenched my fists. When I faced forward again, I could see the police station off in the distance and Jake's car in the parking lot next to a squad car.

"Blake?" I swallowed hard. Sheila was coming out of the shadows as we drove, and there was a street-light right next to the police station's front door. What if we got that close and she appeared, oozing out of the darkness like waves on a stormy sea? What if she slithered out and grabbed Treacle or one of the other cats and devoured them right in front of me?

"Hold on," Blake said. I braced myself. He flipped on the siren and planted his rolling red light on the top of the car. My head flew back into the seat as he hit the gas and the car went speeding toward the station. "Get ready to bail out."

"You guys ready?" I looked over my shoulder.

"Ready!" Treacle said.

"If we must run, I'm ready!" Marshmallow replied.

"Run? Where are we running to?" Peanut Butter asked.

"Just stick with me," Treacle said. *"And keep up."*

"I can keep up," Peanut Butter said. *"I can keep up for sure."*

"We're all ready," I said.

And just like that, Blake sped past the police department. I held on to my seat belt. We came upon the next streetlight, and I was sure I saw Sheila coming into view. But before I could focus, Blake hit the brakes and turned the wheel, causing the tires to squeal and maybe even burn a little. The smell of hot rubber came through the closed windows.

There was no time to say anything. Within seconds, we were slipping around behind the station to the rear entrance at which offenders were loaded and unloaded without being seen. We slipped under the awning, which was very well lit, and Blake hit the brakes.

"Now!" he shouted.

I threw off my seat belt and flung open the door just as I heard the strange grunting I knew from the locked door in the Gingerbread House when I'd gone snooping. I wished I'd never heard that sound. I should have never gone up there. But it was too late to do anything about it now.

I jumped out of the car, and the cats followed me, with Treacle, always the gentleman, bringing up the rear and making sure everyone got inside safely. I could only hope that Bea had done something to protect the precinct; otherwise, this would all be for nothing.

"Hey, you can't bring those animals in here!" Steve Furdeck shouted from his post. He had been assigned to the front desk of the police department for as long as I could remember. We had attended high school

together, and he had been as polite and accommo-
dating then as he was right now.

"Too bad, Steve!" I shouted. "Where are Bea and
Aunt Astrid?"

"I'm not at liberty to say." He smirked. There was
nothing worse than short guys who had a little bit of
authority. And Steve Furdeck was a short guy with a
little authority.

But before I could launch into a tirade of name-
calling, Blake dashed in and glared at Steve. Without
saying a word to him, Steve opened the locked door,
and we all slipped inside, cats too.

"Cath!" Jake called from down the hall.

"Hi. Where are Bea and my aunt?" I asked. But
when I got closer, I saw a look of worry on his face.
Something had happened.

"Your aunt is in a holding cell. She's in bad shape,
Cath. We didn't know what else to do with her." I
gasped. "Bea is in my office. She's not doing well
either. She's doing something witchy, but she won't
tell me what. It's taking everything from her. The
baby, Cath. I'm worried."

I kissed Jake on the cheek. "I'm here. I'll help
her," I said with more confidence than I really had. I
didn't know what I was walking into. What could I
really expect to do? "Blake is here, right behind me.

You guys should discuss the stuff that came back from the lab. Then come see Bea and me. Okay?"

Jake nodded. I thought he was glad for the distraction. Police work was something he understood. Men like him didn't operate well when it came to stuff outside their area of expertise, and this was well outside that area.

I went to Jake's office and found Bea lying down. Her big belly was sticking straight up, and she looked like a rolling hill.

"Sure. Leave it to you to be lying down on the job," I teased. She was so pale I nearly started to cry. "What are you doing, Bea?"

"Hi. I'm trying to keep this place protected," she said.

"All by yourself?"

"Didn't you see it out there? That thing with the teeth and the wrinkled skin?" she asked. "It followed us here. Jake thought it would be best to bring us along when he got the phone call that some evidence had returned from the lab. But then my mom started acting crazy. She kept asking to see Cedar and said she'd do whatever she asked to get her visions back."

"That can all wait, Bea," I said.

"No, my mom—"

"No, Bea. Your baby. He's in trouble," I said firmly.

"What?" She put her hands protectively over her stomach.

"You are using all your strength to protect this place. You don't have to do that anymore."

I snapped my fingers, and the cats took up their places around Bea: Marshmallow at her head, Treacle to the right, Peanut Butter to the left. Bea reached out and scratched each of them affectionately. I knew a simple protection spell that I had used to use as a kid when I was out playing in the woods so that no one would find my forts or secret places. It wasn't anything special, but if Bea was holding Sheila back by herself, with the cats and me chipping in, we should be safe for a while, and Bea could rest. I whispered the spell, and Bea smiled at me.

"I remember that one. For the forts we'd build in the woods." She smiled, color almost instantly returning to her cheeks.

"That's right. I think it ought to work for the time being," I said with a sigh of relief. "Plus, I don't think Sheila can stay out until sunrise. I think she has to get back to the room in the Gingerbread House before the sun comes up." I shook my head.

"Who in the world is Sheila?" Bea asked.

I slapped my forehead as I remembered I hadn't even told Bea what I learned while hiding in the she-shed at the Gingerbread House. I filled her in about everything except what they wanted Bea's baby for and that I knew it was going to be a boy.

"So we have to keep your mom safe. This is probably the best place for her," I mused, looking around Jake's office. Of course, there was a picture of him and Bea on their wedding day. There was a picture of Bea sitting at their kitchen table, looking all pretty with her curly red hair loose around her face. And there was a picture of Bea, Jake, and me that Aunt Astrid had taken one Christmas when we all wore ugly sweaters. I walked over to the picture and picked it up.

"Where are you going?" Bea asked, propping herself on her elbow.

"To see your mom. You stay here and let the cats and me do the heavy lifting. Right, guys?" Each of them let out a meow, and Peanut Butter gave Bea an affectionate headbutt. It made her smile and scratch him under the chin. Bea was already looking better, and I was happy about that. I went to the desk just outside Jake's office, where Jake and Blake were going over a thick file.

"Cath, how is she?" Jake asked.

"She's all right, Jake. Hey, can you take me to my aunt?" I asked, scared to even see what was happening with her.

"She's in the holding cell," Jake said.

"With other people? Jake, really?" I gasped. The thought of my wonderful Aunt Astrid sitting with shoplifters and drug dealers and prostitutes made my heart break.

"It's a quiet night. She's all alone, except there was one woman who was arrested for drunk and disorderly. She's sleeping it off in another cell." Jake shook his head while he got to his feet and walked me to the small cell they had for female prisoners. The men's holding cell was on the other end of the building.

The rattling of the keys echoed down the concrete hallway. The dead bolt sliding open made a menacing sound that reaffirmed my desire to never be locked up for any reason. As soon as we stepped inside, I saw the bars and heard the shuffle of feet.

"Cath? Oh, Cath. Look what they've done to me," Aunt Astrid said as she shielded her eyes. "I have to get out of here. I have to see Cedar. She's the only one who can help me."

"She can't help you, Aunt Astrid," I said. "She's the one who did this to you."

"What? That's crazy. That whole group has been nothing but kind to me. They've welcomed me and encouraged me and..."

She looked so desperate. I'd never seen my aunt this way. Part of me wanted to cry and throw up my hands. She was always thoughtful and in control, but now she was like a kid who'd lost sight of her parent at an amusement park, frantic and scared. But then there was that part of me that wanted nothing more than to slap those witches back into the Middle Ages where they belonged.

"Aunt Astrid, I need to talk to you about these women," I said firmly. "They took your vision. They are the ones holding it hostage to get you to join them. Except they aren't telling you they are the ones responsible."

"I don't believe you," she said.

"Well, of course not. They want you to believe they are just a handful of hippie throwbacks who want to get back to nature and peace, love, and happiness. Well, the Age of Aquarius is over, Aunt Astrid," I snapped. "They cut your hair to use on their sick altar in the shed."

"I know that," Aunt Astrid said.

"What? And you're okay with it?" I exclaimed. My voice reverberated back to me from the cold slabs of concrete.

"Well, at first, I was put off. But when they told me what it was for, I—"

"They told you what it was for and you're *still* okay with it?" I paced back and forth as if I was the one in the cage.

"They said it was for me to see their vision for the

future. That anyone new joining their coven sacrificed the same thing. It's just a couple locks of hair." Aunt Astrid looked at me as if I was the one with a screw loose.

"No, it's not just a couple locks of hair. It's all your hair," I snapped. "And they are using you because you can see into the other dimensions. You are to be some jacked-up best man at the wedding of the Kly and the witch Sheila, who is outside at this very moment trying to get in here at you and Bea." I felt as if I had been running for miles and only had a few seconds to rest and get all this out.

"Best man? Cath, you aren't making any sense," Aunt Astrid said sadly, as if I was the one acting out of character.

"Aunt Astrid, don't you find it weird that Cedar and her clan showed up when they did and insisted on having just you join their coven?" I said.

"Cath, if you think I would have intentionally kept you out, you're crazy. I knew once I got accepted that they'd learn to love you like I do," Aunt Astrid said. I could tell by her expression that she hadn't quite convinced herself that statement made any sense.

"But Aunt Astrid, ask yourself why they always wanted you alone. Why did they come to your house when you were just getting up and then stay at your house until it was late?" I took a deep breath. "You have to see that they were working you over. They kept you tired and off balance, and that allowed them to take your vision." I reached to the bars she was holding tightly and wrapped my hands around hers. "Aunt Astrid, they want Bea's baby too. And not to be a bunch of cool aunties like me. That won't even be Bea's baby if they have their way."

"I can't help you, Cath," Aunt Astrid said. "I can't even see. Everything is so dull and dreary, and there is no life anywhere."

"It's all around you, Aunt Astrid. It didn't go away just because you can't see it. People go blind. That doesn't mean the things they've come to love and care for go away. If anything, they become stronger because they are experienced in a different way." I was getting angry and tightly squeezed my aunt's hands. "The other senses get stronger, Aunt Astrid. They do."

For a second, I thought she understood what I was saying. But as quickly as that spark had come, it was gone, and she pulled her hands away, wringing them nervously.

"Jake?" I called.

Behind me, I heard the key clang and clack as he opened the door for me.

"How did it go? I've never seen her like this

before," he said. "I don't think Bea should see her unless you think it might help."

"No, Jake. I think maybe just a little time and she might come around. I don't care how smart these witches think they are. They are using basic brain-washing techniques on my aunt. If she gets a little more rest, she might come out of it," I grumbled. "So, what is this evidence you had come back from the lab?"

"You aren't going to believe this," Jake said.

"Try me," I replied.

"The woman you call Cedar, the blonde. She's got a criminal record." Jake shook his head and let out a deep breath.

"What? Let me guess. Practicing witchcraft without a license." I smirked.

"Not quite. You might want to take a seat," Jake said. Blake, who was already poring over the new files from the lab and the forensics team, pulled a chair out for me.

✢ 21 ✢

ALIASES

"The crime scene investigation team visited each house on Peabody Street and found a couple of strange similarities at all the places," Blake said. "First, there were strange symbols drawn in chalk somewhere on each house."

I nearly choked and looked at Jake. "Did you know this?"

"If I did, I would have never left Bea alone for a second. The photos came back with them on the houses or on the property somehow." Jake clenched his jaw. "You can bet we'd be having a completely different discussion had I known about this earlier. It would probably be me behind those bars instead of your aunt, because I would have killed someone."

I nodded before patting Jake's hand.

"They don't make any sense to anyone here,"

Blake said, but when he slid the pictures over to me, I thought they looked familiar. Although they weren't exactly like the one Cedar had scribbled outside Bea's house, they were close enough. If I'd had to guess, I'd have said these symbols drew some kind of negative energy to each residence in order to get the people to carry out their ugly deeds. I told the guys as much.

"We also found a couple small footprints—women's size. We are pretty sure we know who they belong to and shouldn't have a hard time confirming that," Blake continued. But then he smiled at me. It was one of those confident, all-knowing smiles that I thought were so handsome.

"And?" I asked.

"We've got a fingerprint. Actually, we've got over a dozen fingerprints from the same person at each house," Blake said. "After talking to the Stortzes, I found out that although the neighbors all knew each other, they didn't ever go to each other's houses."

"Good fences make great neighbors," I replied.

"So the fact that there was a set of prints that didn't match any of the residents was an amazing clue," Blake said before looking up at his partner.

"And we ran that print through the database and, after a few days, got a hit," Jake said.

"Cedar Kolowonski," Blake replied.

"What? I thought her name was Cedar Lott," I

said. "That's what it said on the business card that she gave me."

"Oh, she's got quite a few aliases," Jake said.

"What's she been busted for?" I asked. This was not the turn of events I had expected the case to take.

"That's the real interesting thing," Blake said. "She's been busted for public indecency for performing some kind of ritual in the nude in a park in Chicago. Death threats and violating a protective order. Harassment. Animal cruelty. And she was arrested, charged, and did time for kidnapping a pregnant woman, who was found, three days after her disappearance, locked in the basement of a house that was vacant and for sale."

"I don't believe it," I gasped.

"Now our problem is finding her," Jake said.

"She's not at the Gingerbread House?" I looked at Blake. "She's probably out looking for Sheila. It's getting later and later by the minute. Soon enough, the sun will start to come up. Remember they said she can't stay out past dawn."

"Stake out the house?" Blake asked Jake.

"She has no idea she left something so traceable at each scene." I looked from one guy to the other.

"Sounds good. I want you and Bea and the animals to stay here. No matter what happens," Jake instructed. "I don't want to worry about Bea and the baby while I'm trying to make a bust. And just for the record, I—"

Just then, a huge crash shook the entire police station down to the foundation. Earthquakes didn't happen in Wonder Falls. But pictures fell from the walls, the metal file cabinets rattled, and the blinds on the windows shook. In a flash, Jake was off to check on Bea. I turned to Blake, and suddenly we heard a scream from the cells. It was Aunt Astrid, and she was in trouble.

Blake ran ahead of me, grabbing one of the uniformed officers on duty who had a key for the holding cells on him. In between the sounds of panicked footfalls and shouting, I managed to hear Blake tell the man to get the door open. As soon as he did, he stepped aside for Blake to charge in. I was right behind him but stopped, terrified to take another step forward when I saw Blake's face.

Was Aunt Astrid dead? Was she hurt? Without taking my eyes off Blake, I walked to his side and carefully peered into the cell. I didn't know what to think of what I saw. The entire outer wall, which had held the barred, unbreakable window, was not just broken. It was missing entirely. And so was Aunt Astrid.

"Where do you think they'd take her?" Blake whispered.

"You don't think maybe she did this? Maybe she wanted to join them so badly she busted her way out of here?" I asked, staring at the crumbled bits of concrete and bent iron sticking out of what was left of the wall.

"No. I don't. I think that thing we saw outside—you know, Sheila? I think this is the fun she wanted to have that Cedar was talking about," Blake said.

Just when I had thought Aunt Astrid was safe to wait out the storm, the rug was yanked out from under me. Now that I knew the truth about Cedar Kolowonski—that she was a crackpot, third-rate necromancer who was so bad at her craft that she had a police record—I was furious. She'd dug up some ancient witch for a satanic wedding with an interdimensional *thing* no one had heard of in a million years and was using *my* aunt to accomplish it. If Aunt Astrid was going to put together any wedding, it was going to be mine.

"If that's true," I said, "I think she'll take her back to the Gingerbread House."

"That's what I was thinking," Blake said. "Are you ready?"

I nodded just as I heard Bea shouting at Jake. "Jake, my mom was down here!"

I rushed over to her. "She's not here, Bea. They took her," I said quickly. "But it's under control. Blake and I will go get her. You stay here."

All the cats circled around Bea and me.

"I can't leave my mom," Bea said, looking terrified.

"Bea, you *are* a mom. And you have to think of what a mom would do."

I saw the shift in her eyes as she realized I was right. She squared her shoulders and nodded.

Before she could say anything else, a slew of uniformed cops came down the hallway. All of them were shocked at what they saw. Only a couple had known Aunt Astrid was there, and when they asked about it, Jake handled it.

"This is some kind of kidnapping," he said, and he wasn't lying.

Blake took my hand and pulled me through the crowd of cops that had gathered. Treacle came with us, while Marshmallow and Peanut Butter stayed with Bea. She and the baby would need their strength and protection.

"How do we do this?" Blake asked me.

"Well, I'm not sure," I began as we carefully went outside. I looked everywhere for any sign of Sheila, but I saw nothing out of the ordinary. Nothing stepping from the shadows. Nothing grinning at us with huge, shiny, square teeth. "Are we bringing backup?"

"Not at this point," Blake said as we got in the car.

"You don't think that something that could punch in the window to the holding cell of your police station is something we might want to call backup for?" I sighed. Treacle hopped in and stretched out calmly in the back seat. "You don't look worried either," I said to the cat.

"They think Aunt Astrid is under their control," Treacle purred.

"Is there something you know that I don't?" I asked him as Blake began speeding in the direction of the Gingerbread House.

"No. But we both know Astrid. That should be enough." His tail flipped wildly.

Treacle was right. My aunt wasn't easily fooled. Once they told her what she was there for, she'd come to her senses. She had to have heard what I'd said. Right? My aunt had to know I'd never lie to her. She *had* to know that. No matter what Cedar or Sheila said or what kind of spell they cast over her, Aunt Astrid had to know.

22

ELECTRIC STORM

When we pulled up just a block from the Gingerbread House, the entire street looked like the set of a scary movie. The trees looked scraggily. The streetlights barely gave off any light, making only dim circles on the ground. And none of the houses except for the Stortzes' had any lights on. It was as if they were the only things living on the block besides Blake and me.

"Is it just me, or does this look like an alternate reality?" Blake asked, his voice deep and low. "Like we're in the right neighborhood but the wrong dimension."

"That's exactly what it feels like," I said.

We got out of the car, and Treacle, as usual, went off toward the house on his own. I knew if I needed him, he'd come. As of right now, Blake and I just needed to see what was going on, although I wasn't really sure that was what I wanted. As we approached the house, strange sounds were coming from the backyard.

"Do you feel that?" I whispered to Blake as we carefully approached the fence around the Ginger-bread House. We stuck to the shadows, crouching so low that my thighs burned with each step.

"It's like an electric storm is coming," Blake replied.

All the hair on my arms and up the back of my neck to the top of my head felt like it was standing on end. I knew if I touched anything metal, I'd not just get a shock but see the miniature lightning bolt snap alive as it zapped me.

We finally reached the privacy fence and pressed our backs against it. There were no cracks between the beams through which to see anything. But the top floor of the house was illuminated by what could only be a crackling fire. Except the glow wasn't orange like it should have been but a sickly green color. The stench from the shed permeated the air—decay and illness and unsavory things all lumped together. The smell had filled the small space of the shed, but what was causing the whole yard to reek like this?

I turned around and frantically searched for a

crack in the fence to peek through. I had to see if my aunt was in there somewhere. But the fence was fit together tightly. Not even a small ray of light slipped through anywhere.

"We can't see anything," I whispered.

Blake shook his head and shrugged. "Give me a minute to think," he said.

But I didn't want to wait a minute. With every minute that slipped by, my aunt could be slipping deeper under their spell. Or she could be getting more and more scared, wondering whether anyone was going to come and help her. Without her vision, she wasn't herself. How could she be expected to defend herself against these broom riders?

I couldn't wait. I tapped Blake on the shoulder and jerked my head to the left. Quietly and carefully, I led him to the back of the fence, where I had climbed over just a short while ago. I made a couple of hand gestures to explain to him that we needed to go up and over. He shook his head. I nodded mine. When I turned to pull myself up, he grabbed me around the waist.

"I won't let you do it. It's suicide."

"No. There's a shed here. No one will see me," I whispered as quietly as I could.

"Then I'll go over," he said.

"We both go, or I go around and stomp through

the front gate and attract all their attention all at once," I hissed.

This was no time for chivalry. It was war, and we were both fighting on the same team. I could tell it made Blake mad, but he knew I wasn't going to do it any other way. Within seconds, we were both over the top of the fence, completely unnoticed by the coven as they stood in their cheap black robes around the fire.

"They look ridiculous," I muttered, more to myself than for Blake to hear.

The fire in the pit was growing larger and larger without the help of any firewood. I could hear them chanting in low voices like they had been in the shed. Before I could focus on the meaning of the words, Treacle hopped over the fence.

"*What are you doing? It's too dangerous for you to be in the yard!*" I scolded.

"*There is something going on at the other houses,*" he said, his green eyes wide.

"*What do you mean there is something going on at the other houses?*"

"*There are black candles lit over the chalk drawings of the Masonic symbol you said the pattern of the houses made. Each house has the same design and black candles burning,*" Treacle said nervously.

I took a deep breath. This was all part of their

screwy ritual. What I wouldn't have given for just a couple extra hours to look in my aunt's library to find out what the heck this new twist to the evening meant. Whatever it was, if they were using black candles, it couldn't be good.

I had been taught from a young age to avoid black candles for anything other than decorative purposes for Halloween. And even then, I can remember Aunt Astrid saying to stick with orange and white because they were prettier and more festive, aside from being safer.

"Aunt Astrid," I muttered. I'd almost forgotten she was the whole reason we were here.

"I'm not helping you! Do whatever you want to me! You'll never get me to go along with this half-baked wedding," I heard my aunt say.

She was back! It was her. And she was mad!

"You have no choice," Cedar hissed. "Now recite the words!"

"I'll do no such thing. If you were real witches, you'd never continue on this path. You have no idea what you are doing or even how to do it. Bringing forth the Kly is the reason your whole sect of witches died out decades ago. And it will die out again even if I have to go with it." Aunt Astrid knew how to talk to these young whippersnappers.

"It doesn't matter," Cedar said.

I peeked around the edge of the shack and saw my poor aunt tied to a stake stuck in the ground. She wasn't going anywhere unless I could get to her. And I couldn't get to her without a distraction.

"Wait here," Blake said and inched around the other side of the shack. Before I could figure out what he was doing, I saw Cedar take a long, hot poker from the fire. The tip was glowing white with heat.

"Recite the words!" Cedar yelled.

"Never!" Aunt Astrid replied.

I couldn't believe what I was seeing. I looked around for a weapon, but there was nothing on the ground. The shed was unlocked. I quickly slipped in and grabbed the first heavy thing I could get my hands on. When I stepped outside, I chucked it with all my strength at Cedar. It hit her in the middle of her back and landed with a thud.

She dropped the poker and yelped in pain. I stood there like a cowboy in the middle of town at high noon, ready to draw my pistol.

"You!" Cedar hissed.

The other witches drew closer to Cedar and glared at me. It was at this moment that I thought my plan was a pretty bad one that I hadn't thought through.

"Cath! Get out of here!" Aunt Astrid yelled.

"They don't know what they are doing! The whole place is going to—"

"Shut up!" Cedar shouted. Luann put her hand over Aunt Astrid's mouth.

"Let her go," I said. "This is over. You can't summon this creature you're worshipping. You're nothing more than a common criminal."

Just then, Sheila appeared. Her shriveled face seemed to writhe and contort as she spoke words only Cedar seemed capable of hearing. She pointed at me and peeled her lips back from those big, square horse teeth. I shuddered as Cedar turned and fixed me with the grin of an insane person.

"Very good, Sheila. We'll sacrifice her. If our sister Astrid won't utter the words, we'll offer this one to the Kly."

"What?" I gasped.

"Cath, run!" My aunt shouted.

Just as I turned to attempt to vault over the fence, I felt a strong pair of hands grab me roughly by the shoulder and yank me to the ground. All the breath left my body, and one long gasp escaped as I tried to retrieve it. I was sure I was going to pass out. But Ethel, who had thrown me down from the fence, grabbed me by my arms and dragged me to the green fire, which was still glowing brilliantly.

I couldn't speak. I was busy trying to catch my

breath. My head was swimming, and I couldn't focus on what was happening. All I could see was Aunt Astrid crying and shaking her head.

Cedar was talking to her and pointing at me. After a few seconds, my aunt nodded, and her head fell forward. I tried to call her name but still couldn't talk. My words came out in a raspy whisper that no one heard.

Before I could do or say anything, my aunt started to speak words that didn't sound like English. She cried as she said them, and I stared at her. Where the breath came from I wasn't sure, but I started to yell, trying to get her to stop. I cried and shook my head furiously. Ethel stood in front of me so I couldn't see my aunt's face, but I continued to call her name. I didn't know how much time passed, but it felt like a matter of seconds.

And then things really got interesting.

❦ 23 ❦

HERE COMES THE BRIDE

For some reason, I had just assumed that a multidimensional demon would come from a big pillar of light in the sky. Never in a million years would I have guessed the thing would crawl out of a green campfire. I just didn't see that coming.

So when suddenly I saw movement in the flames, I was sure it was from the knot that was developing on the back of my head from my fall from the fence. But after blinking a couple of times and taking a few deep breaths, I focused hard. And yup, there was something in the fire that shouldn't have been there.

While everyone was staring, I started to push myself backward. I thought that if I could just slip into a shadow, I might be able to figure out some way to get to Aunt Astrid. If I was going to do anything, it would have to be now, while everyone was transfixed by the creature coming from the fire. It also wasn't as big as I'd thought it would be; it was no taller than an average man. This was the doomsday machine they were all going on about? I still didn't see it. But what did I know?

I tried to ignore what was happening with the witches and focus instead on my aunt. Ethel, staring at the thing coming out of the fire with her mouth hanging open in a silent scream, had all but forgotten about me. Now was the time to move, or I might never get another chance.

I scrambled across the grass like a crab to my aunt and began fumbling with the twine they'd tied her hands with. Thankfully, they were no better at tying knots than they were at summoning the end of the world.

"Come on, Aunt Astrid. Let's get out of here," I whispered in her ear.

"I can't. I have to finish this," she said as she rubbed her wrists. "You go. And give Bea my love. And kiss that beautiful baby when he gets here."

"What? No. You're going to tell her all those things. Come on!" I hissed and tried yanking her by the hand. Of course, she wouldn't budge and didn't even look at me when she started muttering some crazy words I still didn't understand.

"Behold your bride!" Cedar cried out with tears streaming down her cheeks as she presented Sheila, who sank to one knee in front of the flaming creature. It was not hard to see Sheila's body trembling. For as homely as this bride was, I couldn't imagine the groom being all that picky himself.

But just when I thought things couldn't get stranger or scarier, I was proven wrong.

"Come on!" I begged my aunt. "Before they throw the bouquet."

"Your bride!" Aunt Astrid yelled.

I gawked at my aunt. *Oh no. They got her. The coven brainwashed her, and she fell for all this at the last minute*, I thought.

Cedar, whose icy blue eyes glowed with the green of the fire, grinned maniacally. She whipped her head in my direction, but I couldn't be sure she saw me as I hid behind my aunt.

All the other witches were staring at the spectacle —all except one. Ethel caught me standing behind my aunt and, like a rhino charging to put out a brush fire, came stomping in my direction.

The sudden movement must not have been part of the program. The fire beast arched its back, let out a high-pitched scream that was more like a girly whine than anything else, and, with three big chomps, ate Sheila.

Cedar began screaming and whirled around to square off with my aunt. Aunt Astrid, whose hands were free now, pushed me back and stood tall and unafraid. I'd never seen her look like this before. The green flames in the firepit whipped around like a cat's tail when it was just about to pounce. As soon as I thought of a cat, I had a brilliant idea.

"Treacle!" I called to him. Within seconds, he was in view on the top of the fence, his green eyes flashing. *"Go to the other houses where you saw the candles! Knock them all down! Get them close to anything that might burn! Get your friends to help! Come back to me as soon as you are done! And BE CAREFUL!"*

Before I could take a breath, he was gone. I turned back around to see Ethel in my face—literally. She gave me a headbutt that knocked me to the ground.

I was getting really tired of this, and although I was not athletically inclined and couldn't do any kind of female superhero moves or run up the side of a wall, I could kick. And that was what I did. I kicked at Ethel like I was a Rockette, and I didn't stop. No matter how much my thighs and calves started to burn, no matter how painful it felt in my abdomen to keep my legs moving, I didn't stop. If she got hold of one ankle, I kicked at her fingers. When she let go, I went for her knees. I didn't stop until she begged me to take her hands.

The thing that had just stretched its mouth open and swallowed up Sheila had now focused its attention on Ethel. It had her by the leg and was slowly pulling her toward its open maw. I grabbed her hands and pulled her toward me while I was still on the ground. Ethel was crying, but no words came out of her mouth.

"Don't let go!" I shouted.

"I'm sorry," she blubbered. "I'm sorry."

I pulled as hard as I could, but I was no match for the green flame demon that was pulling her by the leg. With one last tug, Ethel disappeared into the creature's yawning, fiery mouth.

When I got to my feet, I turned toward my aunt, who was muttering something with her eyes closed. I didn't know if this whole ordeal had brought her vision back or if Cedar had removed the veil that was preventing her from seeing the other dimensions around her. All I knew was that in the midst of all this chaos, Aunt Astrid stood tall, proud, and fierce.

The smell of smoke was growing more and more noticeable. It wasn't from the bonfire. I looked toward the street and saw the glow of fire from the nearby houses. Treacle had done it. Now I just wanted to make sure he'd made it out okay.

"You don't know what you've done!" Aunt Astrid yelled at Cedar. "You thought you were being slick by sneaking into my life the way you did. Did you really believe I'd sacrifice my family for you? For this?"

"You don't have any choice," Cedar spat.

"That's the thing stupid people like you always think—that people don't have a choice. Well, we do. And I've made my choice."

With that, my Aunt Astrid screamed at the top of her voice words I'd never heard before. And with a clap of her hands, she was gone.

"No!" I screamed. My eyes instantly filled with tears, and I was ready to take a bite out of Cedar myself. What had Astrid done? Why would she go and leave us like this?

The Kly, which was supposed to bring about the end of the world, began to shrivel up like a piece of burnt bacon. Cedar became a stuttering mess as she watched her insane plan go literally up in smoke.

"Get the statue of the Sect of Symmetry! Get it from the shed!" she screamed at Hannah, who had been standing off to the side through the whole ordeal. "You heard me! Go get it!"

Hannah shook her head and pointed to the statue, which was lying on the ground. It was what I'd awkwardly tossed at Cedar, hitting her in the back. She gasped and picked it up, holding it to her while she looked around nervously.

"Cedar? The Kly ate Sheila," Hannah said.

"And Ethel," Luann added through a cascade of tears.

"And your collection of houses is on fire," I added, pointing toward the street.

I probably shouldn't have said anything to her. She whirled around and hissed at me before taking off toward the front gate. But before she could get to it, Blake stepped out of the shadows and blocked her way. She ran right into him and bounced backward, tripping over her own feet and falling hard on her back end. The statue of the Sect of Symmetry broke into a couple pieces when it hit the ground. I was glad. It was a horrible figure.

Just then, as I heard Cedar start to cry, I saw my favorite black cat hop up onto the fence. He looked a little dusty but otherwise unharmed.

"Aunt Astrid is gone," I said telepathically.

"No," Treacle replied.

"What am I going to do?" I stared at my feline as the reality of what had just happened sank in. The fire that had been green was now nothing but a few pitiful embers being licked by small, unimpressive tongues of flame. *"How am I going to tell Bea her mom won't see the baby? How am I going to tell her that?"*

As I turned to Blake, I heard the impressive

honking horns of the fire trucks, which were so loud they shook the ground as the trucks pulled up all along Peabody Street. Blake reached down, yanked Cedar up by the wrist, and began to read her her rights as he led her out the gate and toward the front yard.

"What am I going to do?" I looked back at my cat and shook my head.

The real terror of what had just happened hadn't settled into my bones yet. And I didn't mean the Kly. That had been bad. It had indeed eaten Sheila. Three bites, and she was gone. But the terror I was feeling was because my aunt was gone, and once again, it was because I had been in trouble. Just like with my mother.

Treacle was looking at me, but then something else behind me caught his eye. His tail whipped, but he said nothing. I turned around.

"Aunt Astrid!" I shouted and threw my arms around her. She was smiling through the black smudges of dirt on her cheeks. When I felt her arms around me, I started to cry.

"It's all right, honey. I'm right here." She smoothed my hair.

"What happened? I thought you sacrificed your-self to save us," I blubbered as I kissed her on the cheek.

"Well, you know I would have," she said. "The problem with girls like Cedar is they make big, grandiose plans and forget that a simple sleight of hand might be all that's necessary."

Aunt Astrid cleared her throat as she slipped her arm through mine. We walked out of the yard just as half a dozen uniformed cops swarmed in to round up the rest of the Sect of Symmetry.

"I don't follow."

"I didn't have my vision, but I still knew a couple of tricks like relocation." Aunt Astrid smiled. "I just teleported myself to the corner of the yard. Cedar was too swept up in all of it. She didn't see me."

"Do you have your vision now?" I asked.

"It's coming back, thank goodness." She sighed.

I told her Bea was at the police station with Jake and that Blake had Cedar under arrest.

We quickly got out of the way to let the firemen and police do their jobs. The entire area was cordoned off. Down the street, the last living people that weren't witches, Ken and Liane Stortz, were standing on the sidewalk and staring at their home, which was flanked by two burning buildings.

"We should help them," Aunt Astrid said, and I couldn't have agreed more.

We held hands as we discreetly chanted to the wind to keep the flames from touching their house. It was kind of funny to watch how the wind worked hard to wave the flames this way and that, making the Stortzes sway in time with the gusts. But the scene was still desolate. They were the only people on the block who hadn't been touched by the Sect of Symmetry, and they had narrowly escaped with their lives. They deserved to have their house spared.

I saw Blake's car and assumed he was still dealing with Cedar, perhaps questioning her, or maybe he'd gone to collect the rest of the coven and make sure the police kept them separated. Not that I thought any of them could do any more harm.

"We better get to the police station and collect Bea," I said. "She's probably worried sick. And in her condition, it doesn't take much for her to be upset."

"You're right," Aunt Astrid said. "Do you think we can get one of these officers to give us a lift back to the station?"

"I don't know why not."

I happened to glance between a fire truck and the fire chief's car and saw Blake's car still parked between them. The driver's-side door was open, and as I looked more closely, I saw that the passenger-side door was open too.

"What's the matter?" Aunt Astrid asked.

I didn't say anything as I pointed to Blake's car. I let go of my aunt's arm and headed toward the beat-up old sedan. I looked inside, but no one was in it. I swallowed hard and looked around. Firemen hustled back and forth with hoses, sending arcs of water high into the air to fall on the fires consuming the coven's hiding places. There was no sign of Blake or Cedar.

Carefully, I walked around the car and nearly tripped over Blake's leg. He was lying on the ground, hidden by the curb, with a bloody goose egg on the side of his head.

Cedar was nowhere to be found.

❦ 24 ❦

MASTER MANIPULATOR

"Blake!" I shouted.

Aunt Astrid hurried to us and peeked over my shoulder as I got down on my knees next to him. The concrete bit through my pants and dug into my flesh as I tried to get close to him. My other knee became cold and wet from the grass I was partially kneeling on. There was no good way to get close to Blake. All I could think was *Don't move him if he has a head injury.* But I couldn't just leave him there. If only Bea was with us, she'd be able to tell if his aura was flowing freely or if broken bones or destroyed nerves were getting in the way.

"Is he breathing?" my aunt asked.

"Yes. Yes, he is." I gently stroked his face, which was still warm. "Blake? What happened to you? Wake up. Oh, please wake up."

After a few horrifying seconds, his eyes fluttered. At first, all I saw were the whites as his eyes rolled around, but finally, they opened, and I could tell he recognized me right away.

"This is embarrassing," he said as he raised his hand to touch the lump on his head. The pain made him wince.

"What happened? Where's Cedar?" I asked as I struggled to get Blake to his feet.

"I don't know. The last thing I remember is trying to get that statue from her. She somehow cracked me against the head with it, and down I went." He swallowed hard as he looked inside his car. "I've got to put an APB out on her. She's a loose cannon."

"Yeah, and then you're going to go with one of these EMTs to the hospital," I said.

"We've got to catch her. Cath, she's dangerous," Blake said as he sat down on the passenger's seat and picked up his radio to call in to the station.

"Blake Samberg, you let those men take a look at your head," Aunt Astrid ordered. "Or else I'll have to ban you from the café for one year."

A slight grin tickled the right corner of his lips, and he reluctantly nodded. Aunt Astrid hurried over to the EMTs to inform them Blake had been hurt.

"You are lucky I was here," I said.

"I am," Blake said. "How is your aunt?"

"She's just fine. But now we've got to worry about Cedar. Do you think she's still around here some-where? Do you think she'll try anything?" I asked after Blake called in to the station to report on Cedar Kolowonski, aka Cedar Lott, who was on the run.

"I don't think so. It isn't like she can blend into a crowd. They'll find her." Blake carefully got out of the car.

I could tell his head was really hurting, and I was glad that he'd be going to the hospital, where not only could they look him over, but he could get a little rest.

We walked to the ambulance, and the EMT knew Blake by name. Blake hopped up on the tailgate of the open ambulance and told the tech what had happened. It took a few seconds for the man to tell Blake he would need X-rays and that he'd probably have to stay overnight.

"I'll come see you first thing in the morning," I promised.

"Take my car." Blake handed me the keys. "Get some rest yourself."

"We'll go pick up Bea and then head home. Do what the doctor tells you, and don't bore him with facts about primitive medical procedures like leeches or eating arsenic." I winked.

Before I could turn away, Blake took me by the

hand and pulled me to him. He kissed me in front of the EMT, my aunt, and all the firemen, who were thankfully busy putting out the fires. By the time he let me go and I was walking back to his car, my cheeks were as bright red as the fire trucks.

"What a night," I said to my aunt, who was grinning at me as if she was picking out a day in May for a wedding to take place. "Oh, stop. Let's go get Bea."

"I didn't say a word," Aunt Astrid replied.

We drove to the police station, and the place was as active as Peabody Street, with emergency city construction crews sizing up the damage to the part of the building where Sheila had knocked in the barred window. It had to get fixed immediately.

"Look at this mess," I said.

"What a shame. All this time now to be wasted because of those witches," Aunt Astrid said. "And don't think I'm not just mortified that I had to be kept in that cell. I'll never live it down. Never in a million years."

"Aunt Astrid, you were not yourself. Those women had done something to you when they cut your hair," I said as I gently pulled a few of the blond and silvery-gray strands.

"They snuck in, Cath. I never had any desire to join another coven. Some of them are rather prestigious and exclusive, and I know they would be thrilled to have the Greenstone name in their registry," she said, her chin held high. "Why, the Rothchilds, just a stone's throw away from being blood-sucking vampires and quite backward in their thinking, will pop up out of nowhere every few years to ask me if I'd be interested in joining their coven. Talk about wanting world domination. I hate to break it to Cedar, but she's way behind the curve."

"Really?" I asked.

"Oh yes. But I always thought our little group of three, here in Wonder Falls, was just perfect." She smiled.

"But why did you want to spend so much time with them? Why did you let them cut your hair? You said it was nice to be with other witches, like Bea and I weren't nice to be around."

I hadn't meant to be rude to my aunt, but I couldn't understand why she had thought the Sect was so wonderful when they had given me the heebie-jeebies the first time I'd met them. Aunt Astrid was usually such a keen judge of character.

"At first, I thought they were pleasant. To be honest, Cath, I thought it was nice to have found another group of women who shared our special gifts. We are, after all, not like other people." She winked at me. "But then I started to hear them say strange things, like 'seeking revenge,' and they didn't have any real gifts other than perhaps the gift of persuasion. Cedar was a smooth talker, if nothing else."

I shook my head as we drove. "Did they ever tell you what they had planned for Bea?"

"No. They told me what they had planned for you," Aunt Astrid said, her eyebrows pinched together. "What did they say about Bea?"

My chest tightened as I told her what I'd heard them saying about Bea and the baby. Just the thought of anyone hurting that baby—or any baby—made my heart break.

"Oh, Cath. I didn't know any of that," Aunt Astrid said as tears filled her eyes. "Sadly, I was under the assumption that they were going to invite me into the coven then Bea. Cedar and Ethel had told me that there was no room for you."

"Nice," I replied, not at all surprised.

"It wasn't until later, when I asked why you wouldn't be allowed to join, that I realized that they didn't know you had the gift of telepathy with animals," Aunt Astrid said as she folded her hands in her lap. "I thought it had been an oversight, that perhaps they hadn't read the Greenstone history where the lineage of our gifts is recorded. But it became apparent, only after it was too late to turn back, that they were only using me to bring the Kly to this dimension. That demon could see me like I was a lighthouse on a stormy sea. Once he caught sight of me, he'd follow me no matter where I went, devouring everything in his sight."

"But we stopped them." I patted my aunt's hand as we pulled into the police station. "What kind of power did Cedar have? Actually, now that I think about it, what powers did any of them have? I don't recall there being a display of any kind of witchy power from any of them. I mean, they wore those cheap robes, and the Gingerbread House was decorated on the inside with cheap novelty décor. It was all rather embarrassing."

"Funny that you say that," Aunt Astrid said. "Cedar was a master manipulator. And I do believe she excelled at the power of suggestion. That was what helped her get into the minds of all those poor people on Peabody Street and get them to leave their homes, one way or another. I do believe she did the same to the women in her coven. And what she'd done to me. I barely realized it until it was almost too late."

"So, she wasn't a real witch?" I asked.

"She was a witch but not in the sense you and I are thinking," Aunt Astrid replied. "She might have picked up a few tricks along the way. She'd obviously learned a few things about witchcraft and the history of certain sects, and she was very interested in us Greenstones. I couldn't say why. But she was."

"Well, of course she was. Who wouldn't want to be part of our little clique?" I said after I stopped the car and shut off the engine. "Come on. Bea's probably worried sick."

We went inside the police station. It was crazy inside as they tried to figure out what had happened in the cell where the wall had been blown in. Aunt Astrid was nervously looking around as the morning shift of cops took the place of the skeleton crew that had been there when she was escorted to the holding cell.

"Don't worry. We'll just tell them you had too much to drink and you needed a safe place to dry out," I soothed as I took her hand.

"Promise? That sounds so much better than the real reason I was here," Aunt Astrid said with a grimace as if she'd just swallowed a spoonful of castor oil.

"Mom! Cath!" Bea shouted from the break room, a roast beef sandwich in her hand.

We waved and hurried to her before she could waddle across the room. "I was so worried. I didn't know what to do with myself. Jake had to go on two separate food runs for me. And then he got the call about the fires on Peabody Street, and he nearly fainted from worry."

"Where is he now?" Aunt Astrid asked.

"He went to the scene," Bea said.

"Well, he'll be fine," I soothed. "The whole brawl has been busted up. Wait until you hear what happened."

Just then, I felt the soft fur of Marshmallow and Peanut Butter against my legs.

"Where's Treacle?" they both asked.

"He's fine. Probably already home by now. How about it? You guys ready to go home too?" I asked and received a chorus of meows in the affirmative.

The police station was no place for the cats to be. Before anyone really noticed, we'd all slipped out of the station and into Blake's old sedan. And within minutes, we were in Aunt Astrid's driveway.

But something wasn't right. I couldn't put my finger on it. We all piled out of the car and headed into the house. I stood on the porch and looked around at the street, which was completely desolate at this late hour. What was it? What was I feeling?

"Bea?" I called her back outside for a second.

"What?" she asked as we stood in the open front door.

"Do you sense anything? Do you get the feeling

something is off?" I looked over the banister of the steps leading up to the porch but saw nothing.

"No." She shook her head. "But since I've been pregnant, I've kind of been like a compass next to a magnet. My whole system is off. Why? Do you feel something?"

"I'm not sure," I mused. "It's been such a long night." I took a deep breath and saw Treacle trotting happily across the neighbor's grass to the porch steps. He climbed up, looked at me casually as he rubbed up against my leg, and entered the house. Apparently he didn't sense anything.

Bea and I both shrugged it off as fatigue and, in Bea's case, fatigue and hunger. She went to Aunt Astrid's kitchen as soon as I shut the front door and slipped the locks into place. Why I didn't take everyone to my house I didn't know. It was just across the street, and it would have been safe. Instead, I had brought everyone—Aunt Astrid, Bea and the baby, the cats, and myself—like lambs to the slaughter.

By the time I saw Cedar creeping down the staircase, it was too late.

❧ 25 ❧

A REAL WITCH

If I were to describe the face of hatred and insanity, it would have icy blue eyes and long, almost white-blond hair. Any trace of the woman who had gone by the name of Cedar Kolowonski or Cedar Lott was gone. Just her shell remained, and it was brimming with an even more intense revenge than anything Aunt Astrid had heard her speak of prior to this. She was covered in dirt and leaves as if she'd crawled along the ground the entire way from the Gingerbread House to here.

"Isn't this nice? You're all here," she hissed as the huge cutting knife flashed in her hand. She'd pulled it from Aunt Astrid's cutting block. How long had she been waiting here?

"Put the knife down," Aunt Astrid said with a hint of fatigue in her voice. "It's all over. Your plan didn't work. You didn't bring about the end of the world with the Kly doing your bidding."

"Oh, but you are wrong," Cedar said as she inched closer to Bea, who was still in the kitchen.

Aunt Astrid was half a dozen pieces of furniture away in the living room, and I was miles away at the front door. I could dash out and get help. But if I left, what would become of Bea and my nephew? As much as I hated to admit it, Cedar had us in her power. So I tried to think. And that was a task all its own.

"Cedar, you have no idea what you are doing. Witchcraft isn't something you can steal. You are not a witch because you read a passage that opened up the portal to another dimension," I snapped. "Any high school kid with teenage angst can accomplish that."

"You! You're the reason we are not marching through town now with the Kly wreaking havoc on this miserable Wonder Falls!" Cedar began to shake as she yelled at me. "But not everything is lost. I want that baby!" She whirled around to face Bea, whose eyes widened.

"No!" Aunt Astrid shouted.

"Don't you touch her!" I took three steps toward Cedar and stopped.

Cedar thought this was all just one grand joke and began to chuckle at us. She shook her head. Her blond hair had become wild and snarled over the course of the evening, hosting a wide range of twigs and blades of grass and leaves.

"I may not have the same gifts as you do, but I can read. And while I was waiting, I read a very interesting book from your library. In fact, I found quite a few books that spelled out some very interesting afflictions that can be conjured up with just a few household items," Cedar said. "So don't tell me I'm not a real witch. What's a witch, anyway, but someone who takes simple sources around her and uses them to inflict pain or justice on the masses?"

"That's not what a witch is." I screwed up my face and shook my head. "Tell me what book you read that in."

"I want that baby," Cedar demanded. "You took my coven from me. Why should I let you keep yours intact? You both could have been at my side, but you let this interloper, this fraud, this fake witch, deceive you." She jerked her thumb at me.

"What is your beef with me, lady?" I snapped.

All Cedar did was snarl at me.

Marshmallow and Treacle swiftly slunk along the floor from one angle, and Peanut Butter did the same from the opposite angle, and they met up in front of Bea. Cedar growled in frustration and anguish as she took half a step toward Bea, only to have the cats hiss and swipe at her. Their ruffled fur had plumped them up, and their teeth and claws flashed like the knife had.

"You'd better tell them to step back," Cedar said to me. "Or I'll cut them into tiny pieces for stew."

"I'm not telling them a thing," I replied.

Cedar tried to get closer to Bea, but Marshmallow and Peanut Butter stood their ground. Even when she swung the knife at them, they didn't back down.

I couldn't stand there any longer. I picked up one of Aunt Astrid's pretty decorations, a silver picture frame that had a picture of the three of us in it, and aimed for her head. I managed to hit Cedar in the back again.

"What is it with you throwing things at my back?" she shouted, turning to glare at me.

In that second, Bea picked up her mom's rolling pin and clobbered Cedar's arm, making her drop the knife. It clanked to the floor, where Peanut Butter dashed for it and scooted it underneath the fridge with his paw. But before he could get away, Cedar raised her foot behind her and kicked with all her might. Peanut Butter flew into the wall and collapsed to the floor before shaking his head and pitifully limping toward the library and away from danger.

"Now you've done it," I said and marched up to Cedar.

I had no fear. No worry for myself. No care if she had any trick up her sleeve. I'd had it. With all my might, I grabbed her around the collar with one hand and punched her in the face. She looked as shocked as I did when she teetered back and fell to the floor.

Bea got down on one knee and took hold of Cedar by both wrists. At first, she protested, called Bea all kinds of names, and tried to wriggle out of her grip. But Bea held fast, closed her eyes, and whispered a quiet spell that caused Cedar to lose a lot of her fight. As Bea held her wrists, it was obvious the pain on Bea's face was what Cedar had been feeling.

Aunt Astrid, maneuvering slowly toward Cedar, sat down on her legs as she quickly placed a binding spell on her. Cedar's eyes popped open wide as she tried to fight them off, only to find that her limbs were hampered by invisible weights, and she could no longer thrash about.

"Calm down, Cedar," Aunt Astrid said. "Let it go. Let your hatred go."

But it wasn't going to work. Cedar and her hatred had become one. To separate them would mean certain death. All we could do was bind her to make sure she didn't hurt anyone else before the police could come and get her for attempted murder, kidnapping, and cruelty to animals. She was on the floor, straight as a board and unable to move, when I left the room.

Peanut Butter was alone. I hurried to him and found he was hiding under the chaise longue.

"Are you all right?" I asked.

"It's hard to breathe. But I think I'm okay," he said as he slowly inched his way out from under the chair.

"That was a really brave thing you did for Bea back there," I said as I gently stroked his head. As I lightly ran my hands along his ribs, I tried to feel if anything was broken. Peanut Butter winced but didn't cry out or scratch my hand away. I was hopeful he was just a little bruised. Bea would be able to confirm it.

"She'd have done the same for me," he purred.

"You're right. She would have," I replied.

"Plus, the baby can't wait to meet me. He kicks and bounces in her belly when I curl up and purr next to it," Peanut Butter bragged before gingerly sitting down.

"Do you know it's a he?" I asked, since all of Cedar's witchy wherewithal had been called into question. She and the coven had said the baby was a boy, but perhaps they were just guessing. Or maybe they'd made their prediction based on one of those old wives' tales.

"It's a boy all right." Peanut Butter looked up at me.

"I felt him do the same thing when you entered the room and started talking."

"You did?" I felt tears sting my eyes.

Peanut Butter didn't do anything more than purr and rub his head against my hand. I scratched him behind the ears and told him to remain in the library until our guest was gone. Then Bea could check up on him, and hopefully we wouldn't have to take him to the vet.

When I went back into the kitchen, Cedar was lying on the floor, her eyes frantically searching for something to bash all our heads in with if she got just one chance to do so.

"How are you feeling?" I shouted to her as if she were hard of hearing.

"I'll get you for this," she growled at me.

"Well, let's see. I think we should do a little light reading while we are waiting for the cops, who will undoubtedly take you back to Chicago."

I picked at her as Aunt Astrid called the police. She said, in her sweetest and most sincere voice, that she'd caught an intruder in her home and to please let Detective Jake Johnson know that his wife was doing just fine.

In a matter of minutes, we had a parade of police cars in front of the house, and Jake was leading the charge. He burst in and was at Bea's side instantly.

"I can't leave you alone for a minute, can I?" he asked as he kissed her on the cheek while the two uniformed cops helped Cedar to her feet and slipped a set of stainless steel bracelets onto her wrists.

"I'm all right. Thanks to Peanut Butter," Bea said. "She kicked him. So now that you are here, I'm going to go check on him. Cath said he was all right, but I just want to make sure."

"She kicked my cat?" Jake growled.

Bea hurried to the library, patting her belly the whole way.

I stepped in front of Jake before he could go and give Cedar a little taste of her own medicine.

"Bea held her wrists. It took a lot of fight out of her, and Aunt Astrid put a binding spell on her," I said out of the earshot of the uniformed officers. "I think you better let Aunt Astrid give you and your men a quick spell of protection. Cedar isn't like the Greenstones, but she's got a way with words, and I'd hate to hear any of your guys fell under her spell."

"Yeah, okay. And what was your part in all this?" Jake asked as he let out a deep breath.

"Oh, yeah, well, I punched her in the nose." I shrugged.

"You did what?"

"I know. It's not very witchy. I should have said 'abracadabra' or 'hocus pocus' before I did it. I just wasn't thinking." I took a deep breath and kept a straight face as Jake started to laugh. "I can also say, Detective, that I fail to see what's so funny about the situation."

"Wait until I tell Blake. You know, I expect the Greenstones to do things a little differently—take away Cedar Kolowonski's ability to speak or maybe make the muscles in her legs turn to rubber." Jake put his hand on my head as if I was his kid sister, which was how I always felt with him. "But a good old-fashioned punch in the nose? I never saw that as part of your repertoire."

"Apparently, neither did she." I polished my nails on my shirt.

Aunt Astrid casually put a protection spell on all of them as they took Cedar to the police station. I wondered where they were going to keep her since the primary holding cell was under construction. Well, it didn't matter. Since Aunt Astrid and Bea had bound her persuasive powers and taken away some of the fire in her belly, I wasn't worried she was going to get out again.

❧ 26 ❧

A CONSPIRACY

The next morning, as soon as the sun was up, I went to the hospital to check on Blake. I could hear him arguing with the doctor about the severity of his injuries and saying that men had gone through battles during World War II with more severe wounds and survived just fine.

I peeked into the room. It looked like a hotel room, with a big window to take in the street view, soothing sage paint on the walls, a comfortable love seat in front of the window, and an extra seat in the corner beside a tiny round table. The only thing that made a person realize they were in a hospital room was the weird bed with wheels on it and the computer and monitor next to it that blipped and beeped and flashed while displaying a heartbeat line, a blood pressure line, and a couple of other lines that all indicated the patient was alive. The television was mounted on the wall across from the bed, and Blake had obviously been watching some home-improvement show, which was now muted as he spoke to the doctor. Or maybe it was more that he complained to the doctor.

"I understand, Detective, but we aren't in a war, and we have the luxury of keeping you here until you are really better. That means you will not be discharged until the doctor who examined you last night gives you the okay, and as I said, he won't be in until nine." The poor night-shift doctor looked tired and frustrated as he spoke with Blake.

I could say that throughout our history together, there had been times I felt the same way he did after chatting with Blake. I knocked on the door and carefully peeked in.

"Well, the cavalry has arrived," Blake said. "You're here to spring me, right?"

"If Doc says I can." I smirked.

"It's a conspiracy," Blake muttered without emotion on his face.

I said good morning to the doctor as he left the room and then looked at Blake, who had a big white bandage taped to his forehead just a hair in front of his temple.

"How are you feeling?" I asked.

"Better now that you're here to help me pass the time until my doctor comes on duty." He smiled with his eyes.

"I brought you something that might help pass the time," I said, handing him a yellow gift bag.

When he looked inside, he immediately chuckled. "How did you know this was what I wanted? A Thomas the Tank Engine coloring book." He shook his head. "Oh, but we have a problem here. So, this is what you think of me? I'm only good enough for the eight pack?" He pulled out the pack of Crayola crayons and stared at me. "I'm not good enough for the sixty-four pack of crayons with all the fancy colors?"

"What do you expect? You're leaving in a few hours. I didn't think your injury warranted the sixty-four pack." I giggled. "What did the doctor tell you?"

"Mild concussion. Nothing serious." Blake cleared his throat. "I already got a call from the station saying I was on mandatory leave for three days in order to rest and recuperate."

"You say that like it's a bad thing," I said as I hopped up onto the bed next to him.

"Do you have any idea the mountain of paper-work that will accumulate in those three days?" He shook his head. "How can I rest knowing all that is there?"

"I'm sure Jake will pick up some of the slack for you," I said as I smoothed out his hospital gown. "This is a nice look on you."

"Very funny." He kissed me on the cheek and took my hand. "Jake already called me this morning. I heard you had some excitement at your house. I'm sorry. If it weren't for me, that wouldn't have happened."

"What do you mean if it weren't for you? Cedar Kolowonski did it. She's responsible for her own actions, you know," I huffed.

"Yeah, but I saw she had that statue in her hand. I was going to take it from her, but she just started talking and rambling on, and my thoughts just got a little muddled." He touched the bandage on his head.

"That's not your fault. It's her thing. She messes with people's heads. Look what she did to my poor Aunt Astrid. Made her cut her hair." I clicked my tongue. "But Astrid snapped out of it and managed to put a binding spell on her. She won't be working her magic on anyone else. Not that she knows what she's doing. She's a bit of a hack."

"Yeah, well, Jake called last night and told me that the women they arrested at the house showed not one lick of devotion to Cedar and rolled over on her quickly," Blake said as he opened the coloring book, took out the blue crayon, and started coloring.

"Really? That's news," I said.

"They both admitted that Cedar was the brains of the operation. They had no idea she was going to do what she did, and they claim Cedar threw Ethel Beggins into the fire as well as Sheila Montgomery."

"Sheila Montgomery? That creepy old hag's name was Sheila Montgomery?" I muttered.

"Why? Do you know her?" Jake asked.

"Not at all. I just thought a woman with a face like that wouldn't have such a plain last name. I thought she was more like a Sheila the Prune Face or Sheila of the Gray Skin. You know, a little more witchy." I shrugged.

"Yeah, they said she was the leader and that they had no idea that joining her coven meant they were going to hurt people. They thought it was more like a girls' club with costumes, and any strong witch's brew was that way because it had alcohol in it," Blake said, his eyes on his coloring masterpiece in front of him.

"Will they be going to jail?" I asked.

"I don't know. It was Cedar's hair that was found at each of the homes on Peabody Street where the homeowners died," Blake said. "There were also a couple of partial fingerprints that matched her prints from her crimes in Chicago."

"I guess she wasn't all that smart," I said. "You went outside the lines there." I pointed to his coloring, where the blue strayed slightly outside the top of Thomas's smokestack.

"She'll be locked up for a good while before she's even returned to the Windy City for the crimes she committed there," Blake said. "And I meant to color outside the lines."

"Well, all's well that ends well, I guess." I hopped off the bed and walked to the window to look outside. It was a beautiful overcast day that made the flowers in the courtyard in front of the hospital pop in vibrant reds and yellows.

"You look real pretty today," Blake said.

"Yeah, you too," I replied.

"Come back over here." He patted the spot on his bed where I'd been sitting.

"What for?"

"So I don't have to shout while I'm talking to you. It is a scientific fact that hospitals are kept quiet for a reason. Because it is calming for most patients," he said. "Plus, it prevents the patient—me—from exerting myself by shouting halfway across the room."

"That's not true." I smirked as I strolled back to the bed and hopped up next to him again.

"Do you have any scientific proof to dispute my theory?" he said as he leaned closer.

"I'm sure I could find it." I crossed my arms.

"If anyone could, you could," he said as he leaned in for a kiss.

"You're obviously not that injured," I said.

"I think it's my pride that's hurt the most, since I did let a chick get the best of me," he replied.

I smoothed his hair back and smiled up at him. "Hey, like I said. Cedar had a manipulative streak, and it worked on the best of them." I cleared my throat and scooted a little closer.

That was when Blake slipped his arm around my waist and pulled me to him. "I wasn't talking about her," he said and kissed me once more.

27

DEMON BABIES

"I don't understand any of it," I said to my aunt before taking a big bite from my everything bagel with cream cheese and cucumbers.

We had all slept in at her house. I was the last to wake up after smelling coffee brewing. Now we were in the library, eating brunch while reshelving the books Cedar had torn through in her attempt to find something she might understand and use against us.

"What's to understand?" Aunt Astrid said as she sat on the chaise longue, her hair clipped back in a French twist. She was wearing the satiny muumuu that made her look so elegant.

"Well, they all got together to take over some houses in order to revive a dead doomsday cult and take over the world. It's pretty simple," Bea said as she added a huge slab of lox to her bagel.

"Yeah, but what exactly was Sheila? She had superhuman strength, and her face could stop a clock," I said after a sip of coffee to wash down my bite.

"That's easy," Aunt Astrid said. "She was nothing more than an old crone."

"She punched the window in at the police station. There was rubble all over the ground." I swallowed hard. "And you went with her."

"Well, you have to understand that throughout that ordeal, I was trying to heal myself. I don't remember that part of the incident. The next thing I knew, I was witnessing the arrival of the Kly," Aunt Astrid said as she took a sip of her tea.

"I guess it just sort of freaks me out that a woman who wasn't a real witch was able to summon up a Kly and have it eat one of her sister witches as well as the crone it was supposed to marry. I don't get that." I shook my head.

"Well, had Cedar been a real witch, she would have known that the term 'marry' is not always what we think it is," Aunt Astrid said. "Now pay attention, girls. This is your history lesson for the day, and there will be a quiz."

"Ugh." I rolled my eyes as Bea straightened excitedly in her seat. She was always a much better student than me, even in pretend school like this.

"When a passage reads that a pair is to be 'merged,' it doesn't necessarily mean married. It can mean one entity blends into another literally or figuratively. It can also mean that one entity will devour another, thusly becoming merged," Aunt Astrid said. "You see, only a seasoned witch would know to research words like that. Had I not disappeared from the scene, this Kly would have eaten all of the coven and you and me before it headed out into the street to continue the limitless buffet."

"But there *was* a real cult called the Sect of Symmetry?" Bea asked before taking a big bite of her bagel, which held tomato and onion in addition to the lox.

"Oh yes. And the symbols Cedar's coven had were valid. They had an occult meaning that, had the ceremony been able to continue, would have brought about an irreversible chain of events that would have caused a lot of destruction. You were right, Cath, about the placement of the houses creating that Masonic symbol. That was a good catch. I'm glad to see you did learn something growing up with me. Your mom would be proud."

"What would have happened if the houses hadn't burned down?" Bea asked.

"Well, according to folklore, the Kly would have filled every room in the houses, spilling forth onto